Damsel in Danger

Ex-DEA agent Jason Anderson is trying to rebuild his life after being held prisoner by a sadistic drug cartel. With a little help from his friends, Logan Wright and Jared Monroe, he's starting a new business and moving forward. He only thinks about the past during the long, dark nights. It's then that he feels most alone.

Brinley Snow has moved into her dream home. It's everything she's wanted and more although she facing a mountain of renovation work. Luckily it came with the bonus of a sexier than sin neighbor.

One sultry summer night, Brinley gathers up her courage and asks Jason to join her for dinner. They're instantly attracted to one another but the evening quickly goes down hill as she ends up in the interrogation room of the local police. An unknown dead man had her address clutched in his hand. The authorities – and Jason – think she's the key to finding a cold-blooded murderer.

With a first date like that Brinley's not sure she'll survive a second. Then again she's never met anyone like Jason. He's not the typical boy-next-door. He's all man.

And with a little luck, he could become all hers.

Damsel in Danger

Danger Incorporated

Book One

BY

OLIVIA JAYMES

www.OliviaJaymes.com

DAMSEL IN DANGER

Print Edition

Chapter One

BRINLEY SNOW PLACED the last piece of silverware on the table and stood back to study her handiwork. She was having dinner with Greg Henry tonight and she wanted everything to go smoothly. The baked ziti was bubbling in the oven and the tiramisu was chilling in the refrigerator along with a nice cabernet that needed to be around sixty-three degrees before serving.

It was a gorgeous early summer night so she'd set them up on the screened-in back patio. That patio had been one of the major reasons she'd purchased this house. It overlooked a large backyard that she'd spent days laboring over, digging up weeds and planting flowers. It wasn't a professional job but it made the house feel more like home. The neighbor's dog seemed to agree. The yellow lab named Huck was always there to "help" whether she was planting a begonia or having a cool drink on a hot day.

Brinley stuck her head into the kitchen so she could check the time. Greg was late – at least fifteen minutes – and that didn't seem like him. From what she could discern from their short acquaintance he was the type that was five minutes early everywhere he went. A positive trait among several she saw as possible red flags.

Greg hadn't yet been promoted from casual friend to boyfriend and he might never be placed in that category. Brinley had reservations about their budding relationship, not the least of which was although he was a good looking man by any standards, he left her cold as Chicago in January. He simply didn't get her motor running.

Of course that didn't mean it was all hopeless. This was only their second date and they'd barely even touched. He'd been a gentleman and although she appreciated his impeccable manners sometimes a woman just wanted to be pressed up against a wall and kissed.

Hard.

Clearly Greg wasn't the type to do that. When they'd first met he'd said something about a bad back so presumably he wouldn't be slinging her anywhere, least of all against a wall or on the kitchen table.

The back door of her neighbor's house swung open, the screen door squeaking and Huck prancing in the grass. Brinley and Huck had formed a close relationship over the last four weeks, but it was the man dressed in cutoff shorts and a black t-shirt who had every bit of her attention.

Mr. Gorgeous. Now here was a man that could press a woman against the wall or lift her onto a table and fuck her brains out.

To be truthful, Mr. Gorgeous wasn't his real name. He was Jason Anderson and according to a few of the other neighbors he had lived here about three years. Fran, the neighbor on the other side, said he traveled quite a bit and the addition of Huck to the household was recent.

Jason was friendly enough, waving whenever they were both outside and even stopping to chat about innocuous subjects like the weather or if the mail was late. She'd wanted to invite him over for a glass of wine but was too chicken. He was way out of her league.

Wide shoulders and flat abs. Short dark hair. Piercing green eyes. And that scar. Holy moly, that scar on his cheek made him look a little dangerous. Kind of dashing. And sexy as hell.

He was the biggest reason she'd accepted that date invitation from Greg when they kept bumping into each other at the corner gourmet coffee shop. If she was drooling like this over a man she didn't know all that well, it was obvious she'd been without one too long.

Her neighbor threw a tennis ball and the dog jumped up into the air to catch it before loping back to its owner, ball in mouth. Huck was gazing up at Jason Anderson with an expression that could only be described as adoring. She couldn't help but wonder if her neighbor had a woman or two tucked away somewhere that looked at him in the same way. She'd never seen a female visiting but that didn't mean he didn't have one. She was probably beautiful and successful, always well dressed and never caught without makeup.

"You are an idiot," she muttered under her breath as her phone vibrated on the table. Grabbing her cell, she pressed it to her ear, determined to put Jason Anderson out of her mind.

"Hello?"

"Brinley? It's Greg. I'm afraid I have bad news."

"I can barely hear you. You're going to have to speak up a

little."

Greg said something she couldn't quite make out and then the background noise switched off.

"Is that better? I was listening to the radio in my car."

"Much better. What's the bad news?" she asked, although she had a pretty decent idea what it was if he was still in his car when he was supposed to be here. She shouldn't feel so relieved either but she did.

"I can't make it. There's an emergency at work that I need to deal with. I hope you understand."

Of course she did. Although now she was going to have to eat alone. Again.

"It's okay, Greg. I do understand."

Maybe this was a sign from the dating gods that she and Greg weren't meant to be.

"You're a sweetheart. Please say you forgive me and that you'll let me make it up to you this weekend. I'll take you to that new French place that's getting rave reviews."

He did sound regretful and sorry, although anxious to get the hell off the phone. He was speaking at twice his normal rate.

It wasn't in Brinley's nature to hold a grudge. From what she'd seen so far Greg's work was very demanding of his time. He worked in finance and trading although what she knew about that would fit on the head of a pin. He talked about getting up early for the London markets and had vaguely mentioned something about a hedge fund and market derivatives.

"That sounds lovely and I completely understand, although we don't have too many emergencies in second grade unless it's a skinned knee."

"Those kids are lucky to have you. Listen, I need to go. I'll call you about this weekend."

And with that Brinley's phone went dead. Sighing, she slapped the phone on the table and wondered what to do next.

She could sit down all alone and eat the meal she'd slaved over or she could pack it up in the fridge and drink wine in front of the television until she fell asleep.

Feeling sorry for herself.

Brinley sighed and began to stack up the dishes on the table. She was looking down so she didn't see the tennis ball until it smacked against her screen, ripping it from the frame. The ball landed harmlessly on the floor but Huck was jumping up and barking, trying to get into the patio.

"Shit. Hey, I'm sorry." Jason Anderson jogged over and slipped his fingers under Huck's collar to get him under control. "He and I got a little wild. I'll get this fixed for you, I promise."

She picked up the tennis ball and tossed it out of the gaping hole in her screen to the whining dog held fast by her neighbor. Luckily she liked dogs much more than she liked screens. Jason's hand snaked out and caught the ball before Huck had a chance to grab it.

"It's not a big deal. It needed replacing anyway. They all do." Along with everything else in the house. But that's why she'd purchased it. She wanted to make it her own. And the rundown nature of the property ensured she'd been able to afford it.

"Still, you probably weren't planning to replace them right away. They have some life left. I'll get a staple gun and mend it until I can get it replaced."

"It's not nec–"

She needn't have bothered to answer because Mr. Gorgeous was already striding toward his own garage, Huck at his heels. She barely had time to turn off the oven before he was standing on a ladder and stapling the screen back into its frame.

"There. That should hold you until I can get it replaced."

He climbed down from the ladder and wiped his dusty hands on a rag hanging from a rung. It was then that he seemed to notice her table was set complete with linen cloth, flowers, and a freshly tossed salad.

"That ball could have ruined your dinner." He scratched the canine behind the ears, earning a lick of gratitude. "You almost got me in big trouble, puppy dog. I don't think our neighbor would like us very much if we broke her dishes. No matter how cute you are."

Brinley shrugged, her cheeks warm with embarrassment. "Actually I was just taking this all inside. My…friend called and can't make it."

Huck moved toward the sliding glass door to the kitchen, his nose sniffing the air appreciatively. Jason groaned and hooked the dog's collar with his fingers.

"He's always hungry. I guess I better feed him dinner. C'mon, Huck. Let's leave Brinley in peace."

She was tired of the peace and quiet. She could have that any time.

"Have you eaten?" The words seemed to pop out of her mouth unheeded and without any forethought. "I mean…would you like to join me? I made too much food for one person."

Damn, this was what happened when she didn't think things through. He was going to say no and then they'd be uncomfortable around each other until one of them moved.

She really was stupid. Rarely did she do anything that could even remotely be called brave. Indecision was clearly written on his handsome face.

"Sure, why not?" His features relaxed into a smile. "I've got an empty refrigerator and have been eating junk food all week. A home cooked meal would be nice. Thank you."

It was only dinner. Two neighbors enjoying each other's company. No more. No less.

✦ ✦ ✦

BRINLEY WAS A damn fine cook.

Jason had devoured a tossed salad, two plates of baked ziti, three slices of garlic bread, and was now working on a plate of tiramisu that melted on his tongue. He should have thrown a tennis ball and broken her screen weeks ago.

"Another glass of wine?" Brinley held up the bottle as she settled back into her chair. She'd cleared away the dinner dishes and waved away his offer of help.

"No, thank you. One is my limit, although I'm not planning to drive or anything."

"I think you've eaten too much take out, but I'll just say thank you."

"You're welcome."

Despite the fact that they barely knew one another, dinner hadn't been too awkward. He'd found out she was going to be the new second grade teacher at Tremont Elementary which explained why she was home during the day – summer break.

He'd vaguely revealed that he ran a consulting business and that he'd recently left a long-term job. It was all he was willing to tell someone he'd just met.

His plate empty, he sat back in his chair and admired his dinner companion. Long brown hair and trim figure. Not too skinny; she had curves. And muscles. She rode her bike almost every day, coming home tired and sweaty. Tonight she wore a red sundress that displayed a pair of spectacular legs, long and tanned.

Brinley Snow was a very attractive woman.

Jason had been a long time between women. The last female he'd dated hadn't understood him in the least. There had been a time when that wouldn't have bothered him, the physical more important than the cerebral. But that was no longer the case. Now if he was going to spend time with a woman he wanted more than an exciting bed partner. He had to be able to talk to her too.

Huck yawned and rolled onto his side, letting Jason know that as far as the Lab was concerned it was time to curl up on his favorite cushion and snooze. He probably should make one more offer to help with the dishes and then make his exit.

He didn't socialize too much these days. It was almost as if he'd forgotten how to relax and have a good time.

"I can't believe how much work you've done on this house," Jason observed, taking in the back yard. It looked completely different than when Gail Denton had lived here. "And so quickly too."

"I could barely move for about a week when I was done but I think it was worth it. Everything had gone to hell, both inside and out. I painted the kitchen today."

"Mrs. Barnes is getting up there in years and was happy to move into the assisted living apartment complex a town over. Things fell into disrepair and she was frustrated that she couldn't fix them herself, so she decided to put the house on the market. I was actually pretty surprised when it sold so fast."

"It was the location and style of the house that attracted me. Renovating and restoring a Craftsman has been something I've wanted to do for a long time." Her cheeks flushed a pretty pink. "I guess you could say I watch too many home renovation shows on television."

The conversation lagged as they watched the sun as it dipped low on the horizon, painting pink and orange streaks in the sky. The silence made Jason uncomfortable, bringing back memories he'd rather put behind him. He was relieved when his phone chirped and he pulled it from his shorts pocket.

"Excuse me, it's my brother. I need to take this."

"Of course. I'll just finish clearing up."

Jason stood and walked a few steps away, turning his back to Brinley who was stacking dishes and silverware. Westin Anderson could probably wait but perhaps Jason could use the call as an excuse to make his exit.

"Hey, brother. What's going on?"

"It's always something around here and tonight is no different. I could use your help, actually."

West was the head detective of the Tremont Police department. A grand title, but the reality was he had a staff of only three men. All of them were excellent at their job but West didn't have nearly enough resources to deal with everything that needed to be done.

"You name it. How can I help?"

"Listen, that new neighbor of yours… You said something about her at Sunday dinner a few weeks ago."

Jason quickly glanced over his shoulder at the mention of Brinley. She'd cleared the table and was cleaning it off with a wet cloth.

"I did. What about it?" he asked cautiously, not liking where this conversation was heading.

"What do you know about her?"

"You better be going someplace with this," Jason warned, taking another look at Brinley who was now relaxing in her chair and enjoying the rest of her wine. "Spit it out."

Jason rubbed his suddenly aching temples.

"I need you to trust me. I don't want to get into it on the phone but I will say that there's been a murder."

"What the–" West interrupted Jason before he'd even finished his sentence.

"I'll tell you every detail when I see you. I just need to talk to her. Can you get her here or not? I can always send a cruiser to pick her up."

Jason couldn't catch a fucking break. Just when life looked like it would be quiet and uneventful, someone smacked him in the head with a two by four.

"Give me fifteen minutes," Jason snarled and pressed the end button harder than he needed to. Turning back to his smiling hostess, he wasn't quite sure what to say or how much to tell her. Not that he knew all that much.

"Is everything okay?" she asked, her brows pulled down and

clearly worried. “You look like you got bad news.”

Just how bad he didn’t know.

“Brinley, how would you like to take a little drive?”

Jason rubbed the back of his neck as her frown deepened. “It’s kind of late. Where did you want to go?”

If he was going to eat this shit sandwich, he might as well take a big bite.

“The police station. My brother would like to ask you a few questions.”

Chapter Two

IT HAD TAKEN a good five minutes of persuading to convince Brinley that Jason wasn't kidding. At first she'd laughed as if it was all a macabre joke. Then her expression had turned to horror when she'd realized he was serious.

Someone was dead and the police wanted to talk to her about it.

"I'll get you something to drink." Jason patted her shoulder, stiff and rigid under his palm. Her face was pale and her gaze darted around the interrogation room, here and there, trying to take in everything. If she'd ever been in a police station before Jason would kiss a tarantula.

He left her sitting in the gray room by herself, just the lone woman, a table and two chairs, sitting opposite each other. At least there were a couple of windows but the blinds were pulled closed. It was dreary and depressing and he wanted to get back to her as quickly as possible. But first he needed a few answers from his brother.

He grabbed West's arm and dragged him into the hall, shutting the door behind him.

"You said you'd give me the details when you saw me. So

talk."

West glanced at the door to the interrogation room before answering. "I've got a dead body at the Tremont Motor Inn. Looks like someone took a cannon to the guy's chest."

Jason rubbed the back of his neck and took a deep breath to keep his impatience under control. Sometimes West could be a real pain in the ass.

"Do you remember that time I tied you to the ceiling fan when you were five? It was because you were doing exactly what you're doing now. Will you just fucking tell me what's going on? What does this have to do with Brinley?"

West flashed a smile and chuckled at the memory. "I remember Mom and Dad were so mad you had to clean out the horse stalls for a month. Good times."

"I swear I'll do it ag–"

West waved the threat away. "I'll tell you. Damn, you're wound tight these days. You should meditate or some shit like that. Anyway, the dearly departed was clutching a piece of paper in his hand when we found him. It was the address of your new neighbor. Right now she's the only lead I have in this murder case. Hopefully she was a friend of the victim and might have an idea who did this."

A wave of relief ran through Jason's body and he sagged against the door. "Then you don't think…"

"I don't think anything yet. I need to talk to her and find out what she knows."

"I want to be there."

Brinley had looked terrified when she'd sat down. There was no way Jason was leaving her alone.

"If she's okay with it, I'm okay. Let's get this done."

✦ ✦ ✦

WHAT HAD STARTED as a pleasant evening and dinner had turned into a nightmare.

Senior Detective Westin Anderson, who had a strong family resemblance to his brother, really did want to talk to Brinley about a murder. Jason hadn't been kidding and she hadn't given him an easy time when he'd delivered his news. She couldn't imagine knowing anything about a murder in a town she'd only lived in for a month.

Frankly, there wasn't one good thing about this entire situation.

Two cans of root beer were placed on the table by Jason who then perched on the window ledge, stretching out his long legs. Feeling railroaded into coming here tonight, Brinley refused to look him in the eye. He'd followed her closely all the way here when she'd refused to let him drive her, even trying to guide her with a hand on her elbow when they'd entered the building. She'd shaken him off, marching up to the receptionist desk, completely ignoring him.

But of course he knew everyone in the whole damn building and they treated him like a long lost king, fawning all over him. Why they were acting that way she had no idea, and frankly she had bigger problems to worry about.

West popped open a can and slid it across to her before opening one for himself. "As Jason told you we have a murder victim that we'd like to talk to you about. The man was staying in room twelve at the Tremont Motor Inn. Do you know this gentleman?"

West showed her a photo that had to have been taken post-death and her stomach twisted in her abdomen. Ghastly pale, the man had dark hair and looked to be in his mid-twenties.

Her mouth suddenly dry, she shook her head and reached for the root beer with a trembling hand. "No. I've never seen him before."

Placing the photo back into the file folder, he pulled out a small plastic bag. "His name is Roger Gaines. He's twenty-six and lives Billings. Does that ring any bells?"

From the corner of her eye she could see Jason shifting as if he was anxious for her reply.

"No," she said forcefully, wanting this questioning to come to an end. Curling up in her own bed in her own home sounded like heaven right now. "I said I don't know him, and I've never been to Billings."

Sweat had begun to pool on the back of her neck and her heart pounded so loudly she was sure both West and Jason could hear it. Trying desperately to relax, she concentrated on her breathing.

In. Out. In. Out.

It didn't help much. She was terrified. She had no friends in this town and no one to defend her from a false charge. Moving away from Chicago and her family and friends suddenly seemed like the height of stupidity.

"Does this look familiar?"

West held out the plastic bag for her inspection. Inside was a slip of paper with her address scrawled on it. The paper was plain white and the writing in blue pen. It couldn't have been more generic.

"No. I didn't write it if that's what you're asking. I told you I don't know this guy."

Jason's brother wore an inscrutable expression that made her want to toss the root beer can at his head. She had no idea if he believed her or if he thought she was a raving ax murderer let loose on the good citizens of Tremont.

"Would you be willing to give us a handwriting sample?"

In the process of taking a drink when he asked the question, Brinley's throat tightened up, making it hard to swallow the sweet liquid. This guy obviously thought she was a killer.

"Do I need a lawyer?"

"Let me ask you a question," West said instead of answering her own query. "Where were you about eight o'clock tonight?"

"She was with me." Jason had answered so quickly she hadn't had a chance to respond. He moved away the two steps from the window to the table and leaned forward, his palms on the smooth surface, looking his brother in the eye. "She was with me or in my sight since about seven this evening. What's the estimated time of death?"

West retreated from his brother's intensity, leaning back in his chair to put distance between them. "Preliminary estimates put the time of death between eight and nine tonight."

For the first time since Jason took that phone call, Brinley felt like she could actually breathe. "Then you have to know that I didn't have anything to do with this." She stood, the chair scraping on the gray tile. "Can I go now?"

West dragged his fingers through his hair and sighed. "Ms.

Snow, I can't hold you here. You can leave at any time. But I'm asking that you stay. You are the only link to a dead man."

Brinley threw her hands up, tired of the cat and mouse bullshit that this man had been playing. "I don't know him. I don't know how I can help you."

Jason straightened and began to pace the room. "Is there anyone that you can think of that was coming to visit you? A contractor maybe? Perhaps he's someone you met briefly in Chicago. Or a friend of a friend?"

Sighing, she fell back into the chair and held her hand out. "A contractor from Billings? That seems far-fetched. Okay, let me see the photo again."

The cop handed it to her and she grimaced as she studied the still, pale features, looking for any sign of recognition. She was stunned by how young he looked, his pasty skin completely unlined with just a hint of baby fat in his cheek and neck. But she still didn't know who he was or why he had her address in his hand.

"I'm sorry, I really don't know him," she admitted in defeat, handing the photo back. "Maybe he had the wrong address. Maybe he was coming to see someone else on the street. He could have been coming to see Jason."

West smiled at his brother and handed him the picture. "She's got a point. Do you recognize him? Is he one of your perps maybe freshly out of prison, coming to make a personal visit?"

"Perps?" Brinley frowned, her gaze going back and forth between the men. "What does he mean by that? Are you some kind of detective too?"

Jason shifted uncomfortably on his feet. "I used to be with the DEA. I'm retired."

"You look pretty young to be retired," she retorted, knowing full well he wasn't telling her the whole truth by the way he looked everywhere but directly at her.

"I have a consulting business. Can we get back to this case? What do we know about the victim, West? If we knew something about him we might be able to make some sort of a connection to something in Brinley's life."

"Or yours," she reminded him. "Or anyone on that street."

"I think for the time being we are going to have to assume that the address in his hand was correct," Jason stated, rubbing his chin in thought. "We have to figure out the link between you and Roger Gaines."

From the set of Jason's jaw she wasn't going to win this argument.

And she was still annoyed with him. She couldn't forget that either. Except the anger that she had felt earlier had drained away, leaving a little fear and a bunch of curiosity. She needed to know why someone had her address in his hand.

And why someone had wanted him dead.

"So what do we do next?"

"*You* don't do anything. *The police* start investigating the victim. Family. Friends. Try and find out why he was here in Tremont." He pointed to her. "*You* stay out of the way and be available to answer questions if needed."

Brinley turned to West who was watching the back and forth with interest. "So after dragging me down here and practically accusing me of murder, you're sending me home with a pat on the head? You cannot be serious."

West Anderson grinned, showing off the same dimple in his right cheek that Jason sported. "Good news. You have an iron clad alibi and you're not a suspect, Ms. Snow. I suggest you do as Jason said. Go back to your life and be available when we have more information. I want to thank you for coming down here and putting up with this questioning. You were very understanding and polite despite the circumstances. If you think of anything that could help us just give me a call." West stood and slapped his brother on the back. "I was hoping you would help us on this one. I'm short a man who's out on medical leave."

"I'll call Jared and get him to do some deep background on our victim." Jason punched a note into his phone. "I'd like to see the crime scene as well."

"I can get you in tomorrow morning. Meet me there about nine." West smiled at Brinley. "Thanks again for coming in. If we find anything that links to you we'll be in touch."

The detective strode out of the room, leaving her and Jason alone. He finished tapping something into his phone and finally looked up. "Are you ready to go? You've got to be exhausted after going through this. You did great, by the way. You handled it perfectly."

Brinley's fingers tightened on the root beer can as she fought the urge to toss it at Jason's head, in addition to his brother's.

"Since I've never been dragged into a police station, interrogated like a criminal, and then been given a gigantic never mind, it's good to hear that I didn't mess things up."

Her tone dripped sarcasm and she didn't care. These two men acted like this happened every day.

Maybe for them it did, but not for her.

"I can see that you're upset." Jason placed his hand on her shoulder and she shrugged it off. "But see this from their point of view. West had no choice but to call you down here and question you. He would have been derelict in his duties if he hadn't. Right now you're the only clue."

She didn't like being a clue. But she also didn't like being mad. It wasn't the most productive of emotions.

"I'm just not happy about any of this. This guy had my address in his hand. Why? What did he want with me? And why did someone kill him? It makes my head hurt."

"That's what I intend to find out," Jason said gently. "I know you don't know me very well but please trust me on this. I'm going to do everything I can to solve this case."

Brinley didn't want to talk anymore. She needed to be alone to sort through everything that had happened.

"I'm going home. I have a headache."

"Of course. I just need to talk to West again and then I'll follow you. Why don't you wait outside for me? Maybe the fresh air will help your headache."

Jason disappeared around a corner and Brinley grabbed her purse and exited the building. She needed a bath, a glass of wine, and a good night's sleep but she'd settle for two out of three. With one phone call her world had been turned upside down. And it wouldn't be right again until she knew where she fit in this mystery.

Chapter Three

JASON CRADLED THE phone between his shoulder and ear as he poured his morning cup of coffee. He hadn't slept well – again – and it was going to take at least two or three cups to really get going today.

"So what did you find?" he asked Jared Monroe. Jared was a former small town sheriff that had joined Jason as a partner in his new law enforcement consulting business. Currently located in Seattle with his wife, he was a computer geek who could find the proverbial needle in a haystack.

Jason had called him last night after he'd seen Brinley to her home and poured her a glass of wine. She'd been upset – and rightly so – about being questioned. Hopefully she was feeling better this morning.

"I'm still working on it but I do have some information. Roger Gaines was twenty-six years old and lived in the apartment above the garage in his brother's house in Billings. His parents are dead and I couldn't find any other relatives other than the brother, Stuart Gaines, age thirty. He's married to one Lisa Johnson Gaines. She's a special education teacher. No kids. Roger graduated two years ago with a degree in psychology from the University of Montana. From what I can see he's had a series of entry level jobs in restaurants and retail establishments, the last one about six months ago."

"A college graduate and he worked minimum wage? No wonder he lived in his brother's garage. Anything else?"

"From what I can tell from his Twitter posts he liked to sleep late during the week. He has several unpaid parking tickets in Missoula but no arrest record. He does have a car registered in his name – a white 2003 Toyota Camry – that looks like it used to belong to his brother."

Jason took a gulp of the steaming brew, almost burning his tongue. "Brinley's a teacher too. Maybe there's some connection there."

He was grasping at straws but that's all they had at the moment. The connection between Gaines and Brinley could be whisper thin.

"Did you do that other thing we talked about?" Jason asked. He'd hated to do it but he didn't have a choice.

He'd asked Jared to investigate Brinley. And he felt like a total shit about it. He felt guilty about going behind her back even though he shouldn't. He was doing his damn job. Sure, he could ask her but she might leave something important out. Better to have an unbiased third-party doing the investigating.

"I'm working on that now. I'll have more for you later today." There was a pause before Jared spoke again. "Just how personal do you want me to get?"

"Very personal. Money, credit, the whole works. I need to know why Gaines had Brinley's address in his hand."

"It could have absolutely nothing to do with why he was

murdered," Jared warned. "It could have been random. Or maybe a drug deal or robbery gone bad."

Random crimes were a bitch to solve unless they had good forensics. If Gaines was shot for a reason Jason would find it.

"I'll know more this morning when I get a look at the crime scene. The autopsy should be today as well."

"Then I'll let you get to it. I'll touch base later today."

After hanging up Jason topped up the travel mug and grabbed his keys off the counter before heading to his truck.

For the first time in a long while he had a purpose. A goal.

It felt damn good.

✦ ✦ ✦

BRINLEY HAD BARELY slept the night before but she made sure she was showered and dressed by eight forty-five the next morning, a cup of coffee under her belt. She was determined to accompany Jason to the crime scene today to learn more about Roger Gaines and why he might have been coming to see her.

All night she'd tossed and turned, the man's ghostly face from the photo haunting any attempt to fall asleep. She'd never seen him before. Never heard his name. But there had to be some connection. She couldn't rest until she found out what it was.

Slinging her gigantic handbag over her shoulder, she grabbed her car keys and pulled the front door closed. The lock clicked into place and Brinley waved at Fran Kelly, the woman who lived in the house on the other side. She had an adolescent daughter who was involved in several extra-curricular activities that kept both mother and child very busy. The husband, on the other hand, appeared to be the epitome of laid back and mellow, watching his wife bustle around with loving indulgence.

"It's early," Fran called, a visor shading her eyes and gardening gloves on her hands. In shorts and a tank top, she was definitely dressed for the weather. The temperature was expected to top the high eighties today, but then June was usually warm in any part of the country. "What are you doing today?"

"Errands," Brinley replied vaguely. She still wasn't quite used to small town life where everyone knew your business. Her Chicago neighbors barely acknowledged her existence and she'd thought they'd had a good relationship. "I thought getting an early start would be a good idea. I think it's going to be a hot one today."

The sound of an engine captured Brinley's attention from her neighbor. Greg pulled into the driveway and then hopped out of his car, two paper cups of coffee in his hands and a big smile on his face.

Dammit, with everything that had happened last night she'd completely forgotten about him, which of course didn't bode well for any sort of relationship they might have. Nor did the fact that his sudden appearance without a phone call irritated the crap out of her. She had places to go and people to see. All signs pointed to letting Greg down nicely and both of them moving on with their respective lives. Separately.

"Hey, you look pretty today. I brought coffee to try and make up for last night." Greg held up the two cups triumphantly. "Why don't we go inside and catch up?"

Catch up? How do you explain to someone that a dead man

had your address in his hand? It didn't matter because she wasn't going to talk to Greg about it. She wasn't going to talk to anyone about it. Not until she knew something more about the victim.

"I don't really have time. I'm actually running a little late." Brinley didn't want to be cruel but things with Greg were going nowhere fast. "It's very sweet of you though. Thank you. I wish I could stay."

Apparently he wasn't used to being turned down. He only smiled wider and sidled closer, his cologne too cloying for her tastes. "C'mon. It's Saturday. You should relax and smell the roses. I brought your favorite."

He would know since they had met at the local coffee shop. But she wasn't going to be deterred from her mission today. Finding out about Roger Gaines trumped anything else she may have had planned.

"I wish I could, but unfortunately I can't. I really am very late."

Brinley made it sound as if she had an appointment which wasn't the case, but she could see that Greg wasn't the "taking no for an answer" type.

"Just a few minutes? Surely you can spare me that. I'll write you a tardy note," he wheedled, not giving up in the least. It felt like he was trying to bully her to get his way and she wasn't having any of it. "Isn't that what they use in school?"

"I can't," she answered flatly, no longer trying to cushion her words. He'd shown up here unannounced and uninvited. Now he was pouting. "I have to go."

Brinley turned to Fran who had watched the exchange with interest. "Have a good day, Fran. Anything planned?"

Fran looked up at the cloudless blue sky. "I'm doing yard work. If the weather cooperates we'll be out here most of the day. Richard is working on building a trellis in the backyard."

"That sounds lovely. I can't wait to see it."

"We'll see how much we can get done today. Have fun."

Fran waved and headed back to the storage shed while Brinley took a few steps toward her vehicle. Greg, however, darted in front of her, blocking the path, a sulky look on his face as if she'd denied him dessert.

"If not now, then how about tonight? I think you owe me that since I came by here with a surprise."

He held up the paper cup and she almost choked on her retort. He was the one that had cancelled at the last minute the night before. She didn't owe him a damn thing. It was looking like she'd had a lucky escape. Greg wasn't the guy for her.

"I'm not sure when I'll be home. How about I call you?"

He shrugged his shoulders as if he didn't care but a muscle ticked in his jaw. Greg was at the very least frustrated and possibly angry. "Sure, I'll be around. If I don't hear from you I'll call you tomorrow."

That wasn't welcome news.

"Thank you for understanding. I do really need to go." Brinley tried to keep her tone even and friendly even if she wasn't feeling that way.

Greg didn't move so she had to go around him, muttering not so nice words under her breath. She climbed into the driver's seat and fired up the engine before putting the car into reverse. Greg still stood there, a paper cup in each hand, watching her leave. As she accelerated down the street he tossed the cups into her outside garbage can with more force than he needed to.

He was pissed off but so was she. She wasn't the type of woman to give in to a man's demands or his emotional blackmail.

At least not anymore.

Chapter Four

THERE WAS A giant bloodstain on the hotel carpet where Roger Gaines had lain face down after being shot but Jason only gave it a cursory glance. Instead he scanned the room from his vantage point near the door, trying to get an overall feel for the chain of events that had led to Gaines's death. He'd probably never know what had exactly happened but he hoped to come as close as possible.

The forensic team had already combed the hotel room and surrounding area and collected any evidence left behind. The hotel management was pushing for the police to release the crime scene and this would be Jason's one opportunity to see the room before it was cleaned up.

"Defensive wounds?" Jason asked. The room looked neat and tidy. No sign of any struggle.

"The autopsy is today but from the preliminary report? None."

Jason turned to his left where a table and two chairs sat in front of the large window that overlooked the parking lot. Stepping back so he could get a better view, he knelt down to study the worn carpet.

"These chairs have been moved. You can see the indentations on the carpet where they normally rest. He may have had a visitor. They could have sat here. Did forensics collect any food or glasses?"

"One glass of water in a plastic cup," West replied crisply. "And anyone could have moved those chairs. Even the maid, just to vacuum."

Jason stood and inspected the table, worn and scarred from years of use. Any mark here wasn't going to help the investigation.

"Hairs and fibers? Fingerprints?"

"Forensics took out hair samples from at least four different people plus dozens of fingerprints all over the room." West grimaced and shuddered. "This place was a germaphobe's nightmare. It makes even me not want to stay in a hotel ever again. Disgusting."

Hotel rooms were some of the worst crime scenes and for good reason. By their very nature, people were in and out of them randomly. If the average American knew what had been deposited on the surfaces and bedspreads they'd be appalled.

"And he fell here." Jason stood over the bloodstain that had turned brown. "This is halfway between the table and the closet. Was anything found in there?"

"A couple of shirts hung up and an extra pair of shoes."

Jason walked back and forth between the spot of the body and the door, trying to picture what had happened. Images played like a movie through his brain before being rejected one by one until he found the one that spoke to him.

He could see it now. It was fuzzy but he had the bare bones

of the events.

"The killer knocked on the door and the victim answered it. He knew the killer or was expecting him." Jason pointed to the table. "They sat there and had something to drink."

"But we only found one cup," West interjected. "And there was nothing in the garbage like a can of soda or anything."

"Look at how the cups are lined up on the dresser. There's three plastic cups stacked together and one on its own. That says to me that two glasses are missing. Check in the other rooms to see how many plastic cups are normally stocked but I'm betting it's six."

"Jesus, you're spooky. Since when do you concentrate on little details like that?"

Since they saved my life.

"Age and wisdom, little brother. I've got a few more years doing this under my belt, that's all."

"Well, color me impressed. What else do you know?"

"I don't know for sure. I'm only giving my opinion." The events kept playing through his mind, clearer now than they had been even a few minutes ago. "There was no garbage? I think that's pretty strange when you look at the lax housekeeping here. I think the killer sat and had a drink with Gaines. They talked. Gaines got up and started walking to the closet. That's when the killer shot him. Then he cleaned up, probably taking the garbage with him and throwing it away in a dumpster nearby. I'd have your guys check within a mile area. The only thing I'm uncertain about is how he had time to clean the room up. A gunshot makes noise."

"That I can answer." West pointed to an area near the table

and chairs. "Forensics recovered pieces of plastic over here. My guess is the killer used a poor man's silencer to muffle the sound."

"A plastic soda bottle? Our killer may not be an amateur. He may have killed before."

West shrugged carelessly. "Or he watches *CSI* or true crime shows. Anyone with a cable subscription can watch that stuff twenty-four hours a day, seven days a week."

Why anyone would want to Jason couldn't fathom, but then crime wasn't entertainment for him. It was his job.

"Did you find a laptop or a tablet? A phone? Gaines was in his twenties and I would imagine he had at least one of those items."

"I think you're right but we didn't find any. My guess is the killer took off with them. That's why we initially thought this might be a robbery. The manager said Gaines was carrying a laptop case over his shoulder when he checked in."

"That underlines my theory that Gaines knew his killer. Maybe the killer wanted whatever Gaines had on his laptop?"

"An unemployed kid who lives over his brother's garage? What would he have?" West grinned and shook his head. "What is he—some kind of secret spy? Maybe you should check some of your government contacts."

"I will, but I doubt it. A secret spy wouldn't be naive enough to keep sensitive information on their laptop."

West snapped his fingers, his brows shooting upward. "What about blackmail? This kid doesn't have a dime. He finds something out about someone and tells them he'll reveal it unless they pay."

That sounded like a decent hypothesis. One Jason could work with.

"We need to talk to his brother and some of his friends. Maybe he had a backup system at home and we can pull documents from there."

"I've got a call into his brother. Hopefully he can point us to his friends. Have you seen everything here that you needed? I'm going to release the crime scene to Stan."

The room didn't have any more secrets to reveal. And of course there was always the possibility that he was way off base with his proposed chain of events. The forensics and the autopsy would tell them more.

"I've got what I need."

West checked his watch and groaned. "Good. I'm supposed to meet with the mayor about the budget for the next fiscal year. He's complaining that the lab costs for DNA and fingerprints are blowing us out of the water."

"What's the alternative?" Jason groused. "Letting guilty people go or arresting the innocent? We're lucky to have the science."

"He watches too much television. Thinks I should be able to interrogate a suspect and get him to confess."

"And the case wraps up in less than an hour. Too bad that's not the reality."

Confessions were rare unless the suspect was trying to trade information for a lighter sentence. He and West exited the hotel room, locking the door behind them.

"Looks like you have company." West grinned and gestured toward a car parked opposite his truck nearer the road. Brinley was climbing out of the vehicle with a purse slung over her shoulder. "I'll leave you to deal with Ms. Snow. I got the feeling last night that I'm not her favorite person."

Jason had that same feeling although it wasn't West's fault. He was just doing his job.

"Do you think she's in any danger?" Jason asked abruptly. The question had been rolling around in his brain last night. He'd gone back and forth between yes and no.

"Right now we don't know enough to answer that question." West stroked his chin in thought. "I want to say no but I can't be sure. Any ideas, big brother?"

"No clear signals. That's the problem."

"It wouldn't hurt to keep an eye on her." West softly whistled as Brinley came closer, dressed in red capris and a white blouse. With her long brown hair around her shoulders she looked very pretty this morning. Leave it to Jason's womanizing brother to notice. "No, it would be a pleasure. Just let me know if you don't want the job."

"Go to your meeting," Jason growled. "I'll take care of Brinley."

West laughed and tossed his car keys in the air, catching them on the way down with a flourish. "I'm sure you will. I'll call you later with the autopsy results or any other new information." West tipped his hat to Brinley before swinging into his vehicle and pulling away.

Jason crossed his arms over his chest and gave his neighbor a scowl even though he was kind of glad to see her. "What are you doing here?"

"I'm here to help."

"Help?" he echoed. "Just how do you think you can help me?"

Her mouth tightened and she shuffled her feet on the concrete. "You keep saying that I'm the only lead in the case. How can I jog my memory if I'm sitting on the couch?"

"I'll talk to West about getting pictures of the crime scene for you to look at, although you'll probably wish you hadn't. They can be quite grisly. Now go home."

She didn't budge an inch and he hadn't thought she would. He was beginning to see that Brinley Snow was more stubborn than a mule.

"It won't be the same. You're assuming that I'll see the one thing that will help me understand in a picture. Personally, I doubt it."

"It's not standard procedure to bring a civilian along on an investigation." Jason rubbed at his temple trying to chase away the headache that was beginning to bloom.

"I would hardly call myself a civilian. You were the one that dragged me down to the police station last night. This poor man had my address, Jason. He must have been coming to see me about...something. I have to know and so do you. You said it's the key to finding his killer."

"I said *maybe* it's the key," Jason corrected. "Maybe being the operative word here. Last night you were trying to convince me that the address was wrong and that it could be anyone on the street. Should I take everyone down to the motel?"

"You and I both know I was grasping at straws last night. I don't know why Roger Gaines had my address but I'm willing to admit it wasn't a mistake. Are we going to argue about this all morning or are you going to admit that having me along might help?"

Their gazes met and held.

"Why do you even want to help? Believe me when I tell you there is nothing exciting about investigating a crime. It's not like on television."

"I'm not looking for exciting. I'm looking for information. I need to know why Roger Gaines had my address in his hand. I need to know where I fit in this murder. Can you blame me? Tell me you wouldn't do the same."

He couldn't say it because she was right. But that didn't mean he was ready to fold like a cheap tent.

"I understand your curiosity. You're right, I'd feel the same. But there's a difference between us. You're a teacher – and probably a fine one – but I'm a trained investigator. You'd be wasting your time following me around."

"It's summer vacation. My lesson plans for the upcoming year are done. I've got a few hours I can throw away."

Brinley clearly thought if she wasn't with him she was going to miss something. Most people didn't realize that investigations were mostly a combination of leg and paperwork. Neither of which was all that fun. But having her tag along would give him the opportunity to keep an eye on her.

"If I say you can go with me you're going to have to do exactly as I tell you to. I mean it, Brinley. If I say you can't touch something or you can't go somewhere I don't want any arguing."

"Your show, your rules. I realize this is out of the ordinary and I appreciate you taking me with you. I won't do anything to jeopardize this investigation. I promise."

"Then get in the truck and let's get some breakfast. I'm starved."

"What about my car?"

"You can come back for it." Jason cupped her elbow and led her to the passenger side. "If you're going to hang around with me it's easier if we're riding together."

He needed more coffee and a stack of pancakes. He always thought better with a full stomach. And this case needed all the brain power he could muster. They had very little to go on, plus the open question as to whether Brinley was in any danger.

Nothing would happen to her on his watch.

Chapter Five

BRINLEY SCOOPED THE last bite of cheesy hash browns from the plate and into her mouth, humming with appreciation. She hadn't eaten this morning, and by the time she and Jason had sat down and opened their menus her stomach had been growling with a ferocious hunger. Placing the fork next to the plate, she dabbed at her lips with a paper napkin.

Jason quirked an eye at the empty plates in front of her. She'd ordered a stack of pancakes, a side order of bacon, and some hash browns. Starved, she'd made short work of every bit of it. "I like a woman with a healthy appetite. Do you want anything else?"

An antacid wasn't a bad idea but more food wasn't going to happen. She could barely move at the moment.

"I'm full, thank you." He didn't appear to be kidding and the crack about the healthy appetite wasn't an insult. "I didn't eat this morning. And I have a fast metabolism. I think it's from all the biking and walking I do."

Jason held up his hands in surrender. "You don't need to explain anything to me. I was serious. It's good to see a female that doesn't pick at her food. I ate all of mine as well."

He gestured to his empty plates. He'd demolished a fair amount as well, including eggs, bacon, toast, and some granola-yogurt thing with fruit.

"I guess we both get a sticker for the clean plate club," she teased with a smile. "I grew up with a brother that ate everything in sight along with all of his friends who would visit the house. If you wanted to eat, you had to be fast."

Jason threw back his head and laughed. "It was the same when I was growing up. I have two brothers and one sister, but I also have a bunch of cousins and they practically lived at our house. My poor mother cooked for an army every day of the year. It wasn't uncommon for her to fix a pound of bacon, a dozen eggs, and a loaf of toast for breakfast, along with a gallon of milk a day."

"That sounds about right. My brother Dan is an athlete and his football and baseball buddies were always hanging around the house and eating whatever wasn't nailed down," Brinley giggled. "I remember the summer he grew four inches very well. My mom and dad were beside themselves."

"I think I did something like that too." Jason chuckled and signaled the waitress for more coffee. "A house full of teenage boys all the time must have been interesting. I bet more than a few of your brother's friends had a crush on you."

Jason had no idea the wound he was poking at. He was a nice man and wouldn't have a clue about her upbringing. The waitress refilled their cups and Brinley calmly poured cream and sugar into hers. It hurt to tell the truth but she'd heard that the truth would set her free.

"Actually, I'm pretty sure none of them did. I was always

considered the homely sister in the Snow residence."

His jaw went slack and his eyes widened in surprise. "I don't think there's anyone that could seriously call you homely. Were you a late bloomer or something?"

Tracing patterns in some spilled sugar on the formica table, Brinley shook her head. "Yes. No. Maybe. I don't honestly know. You see, my sister was a beauty queen. She was a Miss Illinois and several other titles I don't remember. Plus prom queen and homecoming queen, of course."

Jason scowled and set his mug back on the table. "Do you mean like 'All I want is world peace' kind of beauty queen? That kind?"

Brinley had to slap her hand over her mouth to keep from laughing. "Yes, although the contestants don't give that answer nearly as much as people think they do."

She should know. Her parents had made her sit through every one of Dawn's pageants.

"I'm sure you could have won a few if you'd wanted to," Jason pressed. "You're a very attractive woman, Brinley."

A warm feeling in her abdomen took hold at his sincere words. She'd had few compliments growing up so she appreciated them when they came along. It didn't hurt that she thought Jason Anderson was pretty dishy as well.

"Dawn was more than attractive." Brinley struggled to explain to a stranger who had never met her sister. "She has...charisma. That something that draws people to her. I was pretty ordinary in comparison. My mother said that I was born with the common sense and that Dawn was born with the glamour."

✦ ✦ ✦

JASON HAD TO physically restrain himself from marching out of the pancake house, finding Brinley's parents wherever they were, and smacking them upside the head. It was clear their words had hurt this sensitive young woman more than she cared to admit.

Something urged him to reach out and cover her hand with his, so small and soft compared to his own. "I'm from a big family and I know how it can be. One child is the jock. One is the brains. Another is the family clown. Our families put us in these slots and sometimes we get stuck there even in adulthood."

"Dawn was glamorous. Beautiful." Brinley shifted in the chair and stared out of the front window, avoiding his gaze. "Mom and Dad weren't being mean or anything. They were telling it like it is. Dan was a great athlete and got a college scholarship. Dawn won pageants. I just didn't do anything special. I lead a pretty quiet, unremarkable life if you want to know the truth."

Jason had hidden scars he didn't talk about but so did Brinley. Very different than his own but still painful. She was carrying around baggage she should had thrown off long ago.

"First, I think you look terrific. Very pretty. Any man would be proud to have you on his arm." He squeezed her fingers reassuringly and she finally turned back to him, her cheeks pink with embarrassment. There was a soft gratefulness in her gaze that made him want to enfold her in his arms and tell her everything was going to be okay. "Second, I don't think you can call your life ordinary or unremarkable any longer. A man died last night with your address in his hand. That's not something that happens every day."

A slow smile crossed her face and she actually began to laugh. "I never thought about it that way. I guess that is rare, or at least I hope it is for the sake of others. You have a great ability to see situations from an alternative angle. Did anyone ever tell you that?"

Once or twice.

"Thank you. When this is all over you'll have a great story to tell your family. They won't think you're ordinary anymore."

Brinley rested her chin in her palm, looking contemplative, but happier than she had a few minutes ago.

"I do have more than my share of common sense."

"Good," he said briskly as his phone began to vibrate. "We're going to need every bit of it. That's how cases are solved, you know. Hard work and common sense."

He didn't give her a chance to respond, instead answering his cell. It was his brother West.

"How's it going? Any news?"

"You have terrible phone manners," West chided. "Didn't Mom teach you to say 'hello'?"

"Okay, we'll do it like that. Hello?"

His brother was busting his balls and Jason didn't have much patience with it.

"That's better. I do have some news, actually. I talked to the brother and informed him of Roger Gaines's death. He's agreed to talk to us this afternoon. I'm still tied up with the other murder case plus another meeting with the mayor. That man is a menace to this town. Election time can't come soon enough. Is there any way you can make the trip?"

It was about two hours away but if they left right now they'd be there midday. Especially the way Jason drove. There were some moments like this where he really missed having a helicopter at his disposal.

"I don't suppose you have a pen in that thing?" He gestured toward Brinley's oversized purse. It was more like an overnight bag. He couldn't imagine what she needed with something that big.

She nodded and dug deep into the recesses of the leather purse, pulling out a pen triumphantly and holding it up. Snagging it from her fingers, he jotted down the name and address on a napkin.

"Thanks, West. I'll call you when we're done."

He hung up and handed the pen back, tucking the napkin into his shirt pocket. "Are you ready for more work?"

She nodded eagerly, her hazel eyes sparkling. "Absolutely. Where to next?"

He dug a few bills out of his wallet and tossed them on the table, waving away her own attempt to help pay the check. It wasn't a date but Jason was old-fashioned about things like who paid or who opened the door.

"Billings. We're going to talk to Roger Gaines's older brother." He checked himself. "Wait, I meant I am going to talk and you are going to sit there quietly and listen. How does that sound?"

Her full pink lips drooped with disappointment. "Typical. It sounds typical. But I'll be like a quiet little mouse. You won't even know I'm there."

Jason would always know Brinley was near. She was a woman you couldn't miss or ignore.

Chapter Six

THE RESEMBLANCE WAS strong between Stuart and Roger Gaines. Both had a pallor that spoke of an indoor lifestyle plus a slight paunch around the middle that suggested hours of sitting per day. Both had the same hooked nose at the bridge and dark brown hair with a receding hairline. The only difference was that Stuart's – being the older brother – had marched back a few more inches than Roger's.

Stuart Gaines and his wife Lisa sat across from Jason and Brinley at the couple's kitchen table. Stuart was holding his wife's hand while drinking a cup of the coffee Lisa had served when they all sat down.

"We're very sorry for your loss, Mr. Gaines. I know this is a difficult time for you and your wife but I do need to ask you a few questions. Your information could help us find the person that did this to Roger."

Brinley held her tongue as Jason tried to alleviate the tension in the air. She'd never talked to anyone whose loved one had been murdered. Lisa and Stuart both had red-rimmed eyes indicating they'd been crying. It felt strange and a little rude to intrude upon someone's grieving with nosy, personal questions but she and Jason had little choice if they wanted to find the killer.

"It's okay." Stuart squeezed his wife's hand and nodded. Lisa's lips trembled and she dabbed at her eyes with a tissue. "We want to help if we can."

"I appreciate your cooperation." Jason flipped open a small notebook, pen poised. "What can you tell us about your brother, Mr. Gaines? What were his usual daily habits? Who were his friends? That sort of thing. Please, take your time."

Husband and wife quickly glanced at one another before Stuart spoke. "Roger was currently unemployed. He'd been having some trouble finding full time work since he graduated."

"That was from the University of Montana, correct? In psychology?"

"Yes, that's correct. He was planning to go to graduate school but he hadn't gotten around to filling out the paperwork and so forth."

While Jason and Stuart Gaines discussed the mundane topic of Roger's educational goals, Brinley allowed her gaze to wander around the room. The kitchen was bright and sunny, scrupulously clean and tidy. The living room they'd walked through when they'd entered the home had been the same, barely looking lived in. Brinley's own home was always clean but cluttered with books and newspapers in the living room and socks on the bedroom floor.

"So how did Roger spend his time when he wasn't looking for a job?"

Lisa's lips thinned and Stuart shifted in his chair. "Well, that's an interesting question. The last several months Roger wasn't really looking for a job. Not seriously anyway. He spent most of his time on his laptop. Pretty much all day and most of the night too."

That sounded boring as hell but then Brinley was used to talking to people all day, even if those people happened to be short and about seven years old.

"Did Roger have any enemies? Anyone who might have wanted to hurt him? Anyone he may have owed money to?"

"He only owed money to us," Lisa said, sitting up straighter in her chair. Stuart gave her a quelling look but she shook her head, rejecting whatever silent message was passing between the two of them. "What can it hurt now? Roger was a good boy but he had very little ambition since he graduated. The fact is I don't think he wanted a job. When we would ask him about it he would talk about making YouTube videos and making a living that way."

Brinley hadn't even known you could make a living doing that. Apparently Jason hadn't either because his brows had shot up and he was intently scribbling in his notebook.

"So you had to lend him money? But he didn't borrow from anyone else?"

"Not that we know of. I asked Roger and he said he hadn't." Stuart answered this time and Lisa twisted her hands together, the knuckles white. "Roger had simply lost his way, that's all. The fact is we didn't see much of him unless it was dinner time. He kept to himself. Strange hours. He would have gotten bored eventually and straightened out."

"What about his friends? Is there anyone he was close to? Maybe a girlfriend?"

"Roger didn't go out much. He was kind of a homebody these past months." Stuart frowned for a moment. "He did have a good friend in high school and college. Brad Enright. Good guy. We liked him a lot."

Jason scratched down the name. "Is Brad local to the area?"

Lisa smiled and nodded. "He certainly is. He took over his father's car dealership on the edge of town. Enright Luxury Cars. Brad was such a good friend to Roger. They were inseparable for the longest time."

"We'll want to talk to Brad. Can you think of anyone else?"

Stuart shook his head, red streaks high on his cheeks. "Roger didn't share much with us, and I didn't want to pry. He was a grown man, after all."

Kind of. It sounded like Roger had never really launched into adulthood the way he should have.

"Can we see his room? It might help."

The couple looked at each other, their expressions dubious, but finally Stuart relented, nodding his agreement.

"I guess it would be okay. We haven't been up there in several days and it might be messy."

"That's fine," Jason assured the man. "We're not here to judge, only to try and find some leads."

Lisa seemed to breathe easier. "I'll show you up then. If you'll follow me."

The couple stood and she and Jason followed them past the laundry room to a set of stairs at the far side of the house. At the top was a closed door that Stuart opened, flipping on a light switch on the wall.

"Here it is. I don't know how it will help."

The smell was the first thing to hit Brinley. A combination of body odor and rotting food. She felt her stomach twist in her abdomen and she had to swallow down her rising breakfast that had lodged in her throat.

This was beyond mere clutter.

It looked like Roger had never put away anything in his entire life. Clothes, books, magazines, even dirty dishes were stacked everywhere. The only place that could be considered habitable was the desk area and still it was covered with papers and dust.

Lisa and Stuart looked embarrassed and uncomfortable. They'd probably had no idea of what they were going to find in this hidden room.

"You don't need to hang around while we search if you don't want to. We'll call you if we need anything," Jason offered.

"Well, if you don't mind." Stuart looked eager to leave the room. "We do have some arrangements still to make for the funeral. If you need us we'll be in the kitchen."

The couple practically fell over each other as they ran down the stairs. Brinley watched their hasty exit and then looked balefully at the room. "I can't say as I blame them. This is beyond disgusting. How could he live in this?"

"You should have seen the apartment I lived in with three other guys in college," Jason chuckled. "It wasn't quite this bad but it wasn't good either. We never brought girls back home. They would have run screaming from the building and never looked back."

Brinley wrinkled her nose in distaste. "It stinks in here."

"It sure as hell does so let's get to it so we can get out of here.

First rule, don't touch anything."

"No problem," she retorted, eyeing a plate encrusted with something that looked like spaghetti with a layer of green mold. Acid rose in her throat and she shuddered at the thought of what might be buried in these piles. "I wasn't planning to, believe me."

Jason pulled a set of rubber gloves from his back pocket. He'd retrieved them from a case in the back of his truck when they'd arrived at the Gaines home. She'd thought it strange at the time but now it made perfect sense.

Evidence. She needed to be more cognizant of that little detail.

"Here's my phone." He handed her his cell. "You can take pictures."

"Of anything in particular?"

"When I ask you to. I don't have a warrant and I doubt they'll allow me to take anything, so if we find something interesting we're going to have to take a picture of it."

Jason waded through the stacks of laundry on the bed and floor, tossing things aside until he'd dug all the way to the mattress. A white shirt landed on top of the ever growing pile and Brinley froze when she saw a large red stain.

"Wait. Is that…blood?"

Jason frowned and picked up the discarded shirt to examine it more closely. He spread out the fabric and even sniffed at it, making her stomach turn at the thought of doing the same.

"You've found something alright."

Maybe a clue. Something that would tell her why Roger Gaines had her address. She leaned forward over the garment that was laid out on the bed.

"What did I find?" she whispered, her heart beating fast in her chest.

"A ketchup stain. That's never going to come out. He might as well have tossed the shirt in the garbage."

Brinley's head whipped around and her gaze landed on Jason, who was having a difficult time not bursting into laughter. His lips twitched and his green eyes danced with mischief.

This was so not funny.

Slapping his arm, she let out a groan of frustration. "Don't be an ass. I was only trying to help."

"I know. And I appreciate it. Really."

She rolled her eyes and followed him as he worked his way to the desk area. He pointed to the stacks of books and papers. "If we're going to find anything important it will probably be here."

Brinley certainly hoped so. So far this entire trip had been a big waste of time.

Jason held up two heavy books. "Now here is something interesting. Books on forensic science. Gaines was a psychology major, so what would he be doing with these? Let's get pictures of them."

Brinley snapped each of the books with Jason's cell as he sifted through a stack of papers, holding up a few.

"Information about handguns and blood splatter. What the hell? It looks like Gaines had more than a passing interest in criminology. Maybe he was using his degree to study criminal behavior."

She snapped a few more pictures and peered into the bookcase next to the desk. There were several binders and she almost reached for one but pulled back just in time.

"Oops. That was close. Can you see what's in these? It looks like they are one of the few things in this room that was organized."

"I thought you didn't want to touch anything in here." Jason pulled the three binders from their spot on the shelf, sending up a puff of dust. Brinley sneezed as Jason flipped open the first one and paged through the contents. "It looks like information on a serial killer case in Florida. These last pages show an arrest and an upcoming trial."

The two other binders held basically the same items except for different cases. Grisly photos and explicit details were not the norm for Brinley in her everyday life. She was used to macaroni art projects and stories about the family pet.

The picture she was getting of Roger Gaines was turning creepy. A young man who had lost his ambition and had turned to absorbing everything he could find about crime and violence instead.

"Do you think someone killed him in self-defense?" she asked, looking around the room again. Had Roger's mind been as messy and cluttered as his room? "Do you think he stopped reading and started doing?"

"Are you asking if Roger Gaines was studying to be a killer?" Jason shook his head. "I don't think so. It looks like he was studying to become a profiler. Remember, there was no struggle in Gaines's room so it's highly unlikely it was self-defense."

"This is still weird. He was obsessed with murder. And then *he* was murdered."

"The question is does one have anything to do with the other or is this a macabre coincidence?"

"My mother once told my brother that coincidences were only facts not known yet."

Jason quirked an eyebrow. "Interesting observation. What brought it on?"

Brinley smiled as she remembered the occasion. "The parents of Dan's friends all called our house one Sunday morning before church. All their sons had spent the night with Dan out in the tent in the backyard and were now sicker than a dog and puking their guts up. So was Dan, by the way. Mom and Dad had been out of town the night before so of course they questioned my brother. Dan tried to convince my parents that it was just an amazing coincidence. Mom and Dad thought there was more to the situation that they weren't aware of. Turns out there was a keg of beer, and a party too."

"Ah, those pesky facts. They do give our secrets away." Jason chuckled and motioned to the untouched side of the room. "Let's see if we can get a few more of those facts. But that story has a good lesson in it. Friends know many more secrets than family ever does. We definitely need to talk to Brad Enright. My hope is that he can give some context to what we've found today. Hell, maybe he knows why Roger had your address. He might be the type to confide everything to someone he was close to."

"Are we almost done here? I'm beginning to get used to the smell and that worries me."

Jason chuckled, the sound low and deep. "We can't have that. Let's get this done and get out of here. I don't like invading the Gaines's privacy at a time like this any more than we have to."

Their visit had only created more questions and hadn't answered any of the ones they'd already had. Solving this murder wasn't going to be as easy as Brinley had hoped.

She might never find out why Roger Gaines had her address in his hand when he died.

Chapter Seven

JASON CLIMBED BACK into his truck with a defeated sigh. A visit to Enright Luxury Cars had proved to be fruitless. Brad Enright was in Denver and had been for the last week at a sales conference. He was expected back late tonight and would be in his office tomorrow morning.

Warning bells had gone off in Jason's ears when he'd heard Roger's friend wasn't in Billings. Out of town was a good alibi. If he'd truly been in Denver, that is.

"So?" Brinley asked, looking at him expectantly.

He had to admit she'd been a good sport today. Other than the whole smell thing at the Gaines home she hadn't bitched or complained once. The stench *had* been awful. He'd tried to play it off like it was nothing, but he'd had trouble keeping down his pancakes. It wouldn't have surprised him if they'd found another dead body in that room.

"Brad Enright isn't here. He won't be back until tomorrow. We can talk to him then."

"We're coming back in the morning?"

"I'm coming back. You're welcome to join me if you like."

Jason had also been thinking about the creepy books, papers, and photos they'd found in Roger Gaines's room. If the guy was violent, he might have equally violent friends. Add in Brinley's address and Jason was more determined than ever to keep her safe. He wasn't sure she was actually in any real danger but he wasn't taking any chances at this juncture in the investigation. Too many unknowns. Too many open questions.

It all came down to one thing. Jason wanted to keep an eye on Brinley until they knew more about this case.

The fact that she was beautiful, smart, and funny was a complete coincidence.

"Of course I want to. I meant it when I said I wanted to find out how I fit into all of this. So what are we going to do now?"

"Dinner," Jason answered promptly. "Then back home. We both need a good night's sleep. I'm guessing you didn't get any more rest last night than I did."

"Not much," she confessed. "I can't stop thinking about Roger Gaines. I don't know how detectives do this kind of a job. I'd never sleep again."

"I don't usually get this personally involved in a case. Most cases don't have this many unanswered questions also. Most of them are pretty cut and dried."

Jason wasn't being completely honest. There had been one case before this that had become personal as hell. It had almost killed him. And it affected his sleep. He still had nightmares, although not as often. It was a small price to pay to be alive.

"There's a decent steakhouse off the highway. How does that sound?"

Changing the subject seemed like a good idea. He liked Brinley but he wasn't in the mood for a confessional of any sort.

There was something innocent and sweet about her that he didn't want to sully with the sordid details.

He didn't want her to know just how fucked up he really was.

✦ ✦ ✦

BY THE TIME Brinley and Jason returned to Tremont the sun was down and she was yawning. It had been a very long twenty-four hours and so much had happened in that short span of time. Her entire life had been turned inside out.

Jason was right. She needed a good night's sleep.

"We'll be home in less than five minutes," Jason said when she yawned again. "How about we get on the road about ten in the morning? You can sleep in. That will get us to Billings about lunchtime."

Brinley nodded, shifting in her seat. She'd been sitting too long and her lower back ached. A long bike ride would take care of it and loosen up her muscles but that wasn't going to happen at this time of night. The only thing she was good for was crawling between the sheets and spending the next ten to twelve hours unconscious.

"What the hell?" Jason hissed, the truck accelerating sharply now that he'd turned onto their street. Brinley grabbed the door handle in alarm as the engine growled, throwing her back in her seat.

"What's wrong?"

But she could see it now even as Jason was muttering under his breath. Red and blue lights flashed on two police cars in her driveway. A crowd of people were gathered on her lawn including her neighbor Fran, Fran's husband Richard, and Detective Westin Anderson with Huck alongside.

The blood pounding in her ears, she practically jumped from the truck before Jason even had it in park. Slamming the truck door closed she jogged toward her house, frantically scanning it for damage, fire or otherwise.

"Easy there." Of course Jason had easily caught up to her. His hand wrapped around her upper arm, bringing her to an abrupt halt on trembling legs. "Let's talk to West first."

"I want inside my house. I need to see what's happened."

She jerked her arm free only to have West block her path as she made a beeline for her front door. Huck enthusiastically greeted Jason who scratched the canine behind the ears, much to the dog's delight.

"Ms. Snow, I'm glad you're home."

The detective held up his hand in a halting motion that made her pause but her gaze was firmly on the house behind him. It was hard to see in the dim light but it appeared to be undamaged.

"What happened, West?"

Jason was beside her again. This time he draped his arm over her shoulders, pulling her close to his strong frame. Not in a romantic way, but more of a reassurance that if something bad had transpired he would be there. His fingers squeezed her shoulder as if he comforted semi-hysterical women every day.

Maybe he did but she wasn't planning to make a scene. Yet, anyway.

West waved his flashlight toward the front porch. "Looks

like an attempted break-in. The neighbor was outside and saw a flashlight through the windows. His dogs made a ruckus and while he was going for his shotgun the burglar ran off between the houses. I've got men out on foot looking for him but I'm guessing he's long gone. Probably had a car parked a block or two away. Ms. Snow, you'll need to–"

"I want to see." Frustration with not knowing in general and these two men in particular made her yank away from Jason and zigzag around West's imposing frame. She wanted inside her damn house. It wasn't an unreasonable request. She didn't want to be protected from the truth or coddled like a child. Jason and West seemed determined to delay learning the extent of the damage as long as possible.

"Wait." Jason's deep commanding voice made her pause but only for a moment. He wasn't the boss of her, although he seemed used to giving orders. Without a backward glance she pushed through the crowd of neighbors and stomped up her porch steps only to find her front door hanging crumpled and sagging on its hinges. She reached out to touch the large footprint on the finished oak but a larger, stronger hand captured her wrist and pulled her back against his warm body, his arm anchoring her waist. "Don't. That's what West was trying to tell you. They're still gathering evidence. You can't touch anything."

Her fingers curled back into her palm, the nails cutting into the flesh to keep from screaming. He didn't get it. The utter feeling of helplessness. Outrage. She'd been violated. Like a million eyeballs staring at her stark naked. Someone had been in her *home.* The place she felt safe. At least until this moment. She needed to see where they'd walked and what they'd touched so she could bleach any trace of them away. If not from her mind at least physically.

With a free hand she scrubbed at her cheeks, surprised to find them wet with tears. Sagging back against him the fight drained out of her. She was exhausted. Worn out and beaten down by the last twenty-four hours. A human could only take so much and she'd had her fill.

"How did this happen? Why?" The words came out stilted but the detective seemed to understand.

West stood on the other side of her, a sympathetic expression on his face, probably grateful she wasn't going to faint or scream or something worse. "I don't know why this happened, Ms. Snow, but if I were a gambling man I'd say it might have something to do with Roger Gaines. Believe me, we intend to find out."

She drew a shaky breath, hating the fact that she felt vulnerable and exposed in front of all these people. Most of them strangers. "I think under the circumstances, Detective, you should probably call me Brinley. I have a feeling we're going to see a lot more of each other."

"Thank you, Brinley. Just call me West. I need to talk to you about this. How about we all go into Jason's house and sit down? Maybe have a cup of coffee or something."

Needing to be away from the curious eyes of the neighborhood she nodded in agreement. "That sounds good. But I want to thank Richard and Fran for scaring him away."

Jason patted her shoulder. "They can come over and join us. I'd like to hear the story directly from them."

On automatic pilot, Brinley followed West and Jason down the steps and across the yard and driveway to Jason's house, Huck on their heels. Her life didn't feel like her own anymore. Something sinister – and very scary – was going on and she didn't like it one bit.

And there wasn't a damn thing she could do about it.

Chapter Eight

BRINLEY LOOKED LIKE she was ready to collapse. Jason had a feeling she'd been running on pure adrenaline all day and the supply was empty. The feistiness she'd displayed when they'd arrived was gone, replaced by an eerie acquiescence that concerned him. She was sitting quietly on his couch, Huck draped over her lap while she petted him absently, her fingers stroking the silky fur. She'd barely glanced at the cup of coffee he'd sat in front of her, instead staring vacantly out of his front window where a crowd still stood.

"Why didn't you call me?" Jason whispered to his brother, who was directing a deputy to bring in Fran and Richard. "Jesus, I could have prepared her for this."

"I was just about to do that when you pulled up. I hadn't been on the scene all that long and I didn't want to call before I knew something." West grimaced. "Dammit, I was here earlier walking Huck and giving him dinner. I didn't see a thing. When I heard the call on the radio I almost couldn't believe my ears. I got over here as soon as I could."

Jason rubbed his aching temples. "This is a clusterfuck all the way around. Something is going on and we're ten steps behind. I don't like this at all. Somebody is after Brinley and I don't intend to let them near her."

He was shocked to hear the ferocity in his voice, but something about this woman brought out his caveman protective instincts. She was caught in something very dangerous and had no one but himself to protect her.

"I'm glad to hear you say that." West nodded in agreement, keeping his voice low. "I know you said you were going to keep an eye on her but now I think we need to watch her twenty-four-seven. I don't have the manpower to do something like that, though. Nor the budget. The mayor and I had another of our knock down drag-outs regarding expenses. That man is a total asshole."

Money and resources weren't an issue. Jason knew exactly who to call in.

"Not a problem. I've got this covered."

"That's good because this case has me worried. Gaines is dead and it looks like the killer isn't done. Did you find out anything from his brother?"

"Yes, I'm going back tomorrow to talk to one of Roger's friends. But I want to hear from Fran and Richard first. What they saw and heard."

The couple, dressed in their pajamas and robes, had entered the house and were comforting Brinley.

"You can talk to them but it isn't much to go on," West warned him but Jason still wanted to hear their story. He just needed that one detail that would blow the case wide open.

Jason sat down in a chair across from the couch trying to appear calm and in control, at least for Brinley's sake.

"Fran, Richard, it sounds like you had an exciting evening." He tried to laugh to keep the tension to a minimum. "What can you tell us about what happened?"

The couple looked at each other and Fran nodded at her husband who began to speak. "I was taking the dogs out to let them do their thing. I was in the side yard that connects the two properties. Anyway, I looked over at Brinley's house and there was a light that swept through the living room. I didn't think she was home yet because her car was gone."

Shit. Brinley's car was at the motor inn. They'd need to retrieve it tomorrow.

"Go on," Jason urged. "What else?"

Fran patted Brinley's hand. "Richard yelled at me to bring out his shotgun and call the police. I grabbed his gun from the wall while I dialed 911."

"Then the dogs must have known something was happening because they started barking and howling, which of course started Huck doing the same over here." Richard hopped to his feet and began to pace. "The light went out in the house and I heard a crash. He must have gone out the back door because I heard a rustle of bushes and then nothing but the barking dogs."

"So you didn't see him?" Brinley's softly spoken question echoed Jason's own thoughts exactly.

"I didn't," Richard agreed. "I keep saying him but I guess it could have been a woman too. Hell, it could have been more than one person. I just didn't see a whole hell of a lot, to tell the truth. I wish I had. I would have shot his ass so full of buckshot he'd be walking funny for a week."

"I know you would have. Thank you, Richard. And you,

Fran. You scared him away and I don't know how to thank you for that. I'm so grateful."

"Now, honey, everything's going to be fine." Fran hugged Brinley and gave her a reassuring smile. "Now this person knows we've got some loud and angry dogs plus a shotgun. They won't be coming around here again any time soon."

Unfortunately Jason couldn't agree with the sentiments. Someone was determined to get to Brinley.

One way or another. But they'd have to go through him first.

They chatted with Fran and Richard for a few more minutes before the couple took their leave. A deputy came into the living room holding a crowbar in a plastic bag.

"Is this yours, Brinley?" West asked, holding the tool up for her inspection. "My deputy found this on your dining room floor."

"No, I've never seen it before."

"We'll send it to the lab and see if we can get any prints off of it." West sat down next to Brinley and scratched Huck on the neck, getting a lick in return. "The lab is done with your home. They've pulled a few fingerprints and of course we'll need you to check if anything is actually missing, but tomorrow morning is soon enough for that. In addition, your front door is broken and will need to be fixed. I can recommend a good handyman if you like."

"Thank you—that would be helpful."

Jason hated hearing that broken tone in Brinley's voice. He'd rather have her feisty or even angry than this… She just seemed sad and beaten.

West glanced up at Jason and then back at Brinley. "You can't stay there with a door that won't close or lock. Do you have some place you can stay for the night?"

She blinked a few times and then nodded. "I can stay at a motel." Her eyes widened when she apparently realized that would mean sleeping at the motor inn where Roger was murdered. "Or maybe a hotel on the edge of town. Out by the interstate."

"You can stay here," Jason cut in. The poor woman was dead on her feet and traumatized. He wasn't that big of an asshole to send her to some motel where she'd be terrified and sit up all night staring at the locked door. "I have a spare room. You can even have Huck in there if you like."

He thought she might argue but her eyes filled with tears instead. "I think I'd like that. I can't–"

She choked up and buried her face against Huck's fur. She didn't want to be alone and Jason didn't blame her in the least. What she didn't realize was that he'd been in a few dangerous situations before. He wasn't a rookie cop on his first big case.

"Let me walk West to his truck and then I'll show you to your room, okay?" Jason knelt down in front of her so he could look into her eyes. Her lips were trembling and she looked like a woman on the edge. When everyone got the hell out of here he'd let her cry or scream. Whatever she needed.

"I'll have my deputy board up your door, Brinley."

She managed a watery smile. "Thank you, West. I'm glad you were here. I'm sorry if I was mean to you last night. I really am."

"You don't have to apologize. Just let Jason take care of you and I'll see you tomorrow."

Outside the crowd was dispersing since there was nothing new or exciting to see and the deputy was pounding nails into a sheet of plywood over Brinley's doorway.

"I'll call you tomorrow if we find anything." West pulled open the driver side door of his truck. "Take care of her. She looks shattered. I've seen that before in burglary victims. They feel violated. She's not going to feel safe for a long time."

"I'm sticking with her like glue from now until we find this guy. I'll take her with me tomorrow. I'm going to talk to a friend of Gaines. Hopefully he'll know something."

"That reminds me. What did his brother say?"

Jason quickly reviewed what they'd learned, West taking notes and action items in his notebook.

"I should have the autopsy report sometime tomorrow. I'll call you since you'll be on the road. Did you get any gut feelings talking to Stuart Gaines?"

"Not really, although I guess you could say they have motive. Roger owed his brother money and was basically living above the garage sponging off of them with no end in sight. Seems pretty harsh to kill him though when they could have just tossed his stuff on the front lawn."

West shrugged and shoved the notebook in his pocket. "I've seen people killed over a hell of a lot less. A pack of smokes and a Red Bull got a guy stabbed not long ago. If you're okay I'm going to head out. Keep in touch with me tomorrow."

"Will do," Jason agreed, sending off his brother with a wave of thanks. Twenty-four hours after Roger Gaines's murder they had more questions than ever.

It was long past time to get some answers.

Chapter Nine

BRINLEY SHOVED THE covers down for the millionth time but instead of trying to turn over and go to sleep she swung her legs to the floor and climbed out of bed. She'd been tossing and turning for hours – first too cold, then too hot – and despite being near exhaustion it was clear she wasn't going to sleep easily. If she'd been in her own home she would have popped an antihistamine which would have put her out like a light.

But of course she wasn't home. Her house had been invaded. Tarnished by some asshole who had kicked in her door. Had the burglar been looking for her just as Roger Gaines had been? Or was it simply all a not-so funny coincidence that she'd had someone break into her home the day after someone ended up dead with her address in his hand?

Not to mention what her mother said about coincidences…

Jason must agree with her mother because he'd tucked her up into his spare bedroom with Huck sleeping outside the door to the hallway. She was sure she was going to wake the dog up when she opened the door and stepped over him to head to the kitchen. Maybe some warm milk would help her sleep. Even if it didn't, she couldn't lie here all night staring at the ceiling and running ever more disturbing scenarios through her fatigued brain.

Brinley cracked open the door just an inch but Huck immediately jumped and began a low, menacing growl deep in his throat. She patted his head and scratched behind his furry ears to calm him and he licked her hand in gratitude.

"Let's not wake up your human, okay?" she whispered, furtively looking right and left. Jason was as exhausted as she was and at least one of them should get some sleep.

She tiptoed down the stairs to the kitchen and peeked in the refrigerator. Grabbing a plastic jug of milk, she closed the door and quietly rummaged in the nearest cabinet for a saucepan.

"Do you need some help?"

Her heart stopped for a moment and she sucked in a strangled breath. Jason was standing right next to her, illuminated by the moonlight streaming through the windows. She exhaled in relief, resting her forehead on the cool wood of the cabinet and her heart started beating again. Her legs seemed to give way and she clutched the counter for support.

"You scared the shit out of me," she hissed, her hand pressed against her chest. "My God, I thought you were an ax murderer or something."

Jason reached behind her and flipped a switch, the room flooding with light that made her squint and wince. "I'm sorry. I heard footsteps and came to investigate."

She blinked a few times to get accustomed to the light. "Is that how you confront an intruder? No weapon and in your jammies?"

Jason made nightwear look very good indeed. His wide

shoulders strained against the soft cotton of his t-shirt that was paired with a pair of black boxer shorts that did nothing to hide the kind of muscular thighs that didn't come from sitting behind a desk.

Suddenly the kitchen seemed way too warm and sweat was dampening the back of her neck. Lifting her hair to try and get a cool breeze, she realized she wasn't wearing all that much clothing either. Dressed in one of Jason's shirts that came down almost to her knees, she had nothing on underneath except a brief strip of panties. She tugged on the hem and tried to pull it lower, feeling way too exposed.

"If you were an intruder Huck would be barking his head off with your leg dangling from his teeth. I figured it was you wandering the house."

Brinley sagged against the counter. "I was trying not to wake you."

"I was already awake. I have trouble sleeping a lot of nights." He picked up the jug of milk. "Were you thinking about some warm milk? How about some hot chocolate? It's not really cold enough but I can turn down the thermostat if you like."

"Hot chocolate sounds really good. Thank you." She slid onto one of the barstools around the kitchen island. "I know why I'm awake. What's your excuse?"

"It's kind of a long story." He poured the milk into a pan and added sugar and cocoa. "I've got some of those over the counter sleeping pills if you want to take one. It might help."

Jason reached into a high cabinet above the refrigerator and pulled down a bottle. "I tried them once but they made me groggy the next day."

"I'm desperate." She checked the label with a knowing nod. "Just as I thought. They're basically Benadryl. I will take one. It can take care of my allergies and sleeplessness all at the same time."

"I took two. Maybe that was my problem. Do you want a glass of water?"

"I'll take it with my hot chocolate. Now you said something about a long story. Well, I've got nothing but time before this pill kicks in. Is it a secret? Will you have to kill me if I find out?"

✦ ✦ ✦

JASON'S STORY WASN'T a secret.

It wasn't all that pleasant either.

Mostly he went about his days trying not to think about it. The therapist he'd been seeing talked about filling his days with good and pleasant experiences. She'd even suggested that he work on his personal relationships.

So he'd adopted Huck.

It wasn't at all what she'd had in mind but at the time it was the closest he could come to reaching out to other human beings. It was easier now. He'd strengthened his friendships, especially with Jared and Logan, not to mention the bonds with his own family. But still on many nights sleep eluded him.

When it was dark and he was alone…that's when the memories came rushing back.

He poured the hot chocolate into two mugs, his hands shaking slightly but not enough that she would notice. He handed one to Brinley before taking a stool at the island. Reaching into the jar on the island, he plucked out a dog treat and tossed it to Huck who downed it in one big gulp.

"You don't have to tell me anything. I was just making conversation."

Brinley had misunderstood his silence, mistaking it for a negative response to her query. It wasn't that he didn't want to tell her. Hell, if she hung around Tremont long enough she'd learn the story. Part of it, anyway. The details that were fit for public consumption. He'd deliberately allowed the gossip in town about him so he didn't have to personally talk about it.

It didn't hurt or scare him now. Mostly he kept it locked away in its own little box. Just like he had been in that hell hole of a prison.

"It's not a secret," he began, picking his words carefully. "I'm kind of surprised no one else has told you. Gossip and all."

"I didn't take part in gossip. When people start that I walk away. Nothing good ever comes from it."

Jason smiled at her naiveté. "If you control it, manipulate it, it's not so bad. Since the gossip mill tells this story I don't have to."

"Do they get it right?"

Jason sipped at the hot chocolate to give himself time to answer. "No. But that's okay. No one ever asks me about it."

"It was bad."

Brinley didn't make it sound like a question.

"As I mentioned before I used to work for the DEA. During one of my investigations I was taken hostage by a drug cartel and held for weeks. I finally escaped. That's why I find it hard to sleep," he stated calmly. Now she knew what pretty much everyone in Tremont knew.

"That's why you retired."

"One of the reasons. By the time I was cleared to go back in the field I found that I didn't really have the drive anymore. It was like bailing the ocean with a teaspoon. I'd put someone out of business and behind bars and three more would sprout up in his place."

Jason didn't even bother to mention the interdepartmental politics and backstabbing that he'd grown tired of. He didn't have the patience for climbing the ladder that he'd had fresh out of the military.

She set the cup down but didn't break eye contact with him. "I would imagine being held hostage by a drug cartel is one of the less pleasant things a person could experience. I've heard stories about the things they do."

The unspoken question hung between them. *Were the stories true?*

"It's not something I'd like to repeat," he finally said. It wasn't as difficult to talk to her about it as he'd thought it would be. She didn't judge or fake histrionics. She just sat quietly and listened. It's too bad she hadn't been around months ago. "They did torture me but not as bad as it could have been. I escaped before it got worse. And it would have. I learned a lot about people from my time being held prisoner."

Selena, the sister of one of his captors, had told him the cartel had much more diabolical things in store for Jason. He wasn't giving them the information they wanted and they were determined to get it.

One way or another.

He'd been just as determined not to give it as he'd known that his only value was in the information he had. Once he'd revealed it he was a dead man.

"What did you learn?"

Her softly spoken question was a surprise. The few people that he'd talked to always asked about the torture he'd endured. They wanted the gritty details. At least they thought they did. He rarely satisfied their curiosity.

"I learned that there is good in some people. There was a woman there – Selena – she was the sister of one of the cartel leaders. She was kind to me. She gave me food and water. Eventually she helped me escape by telling me when I wouldn't be watched. I wouldn't be breathing if it wasn't for her."

Now he had no idea if she was dead or alive. She's disappeared the same night he'd escaped and hadn't been heard from since.

"Anything else?"

Somehow her hand had crossed the island and was now resting on his. He turned his so their fingers tangled together, her warmth seeping into his cold, lonely soul.

"I also learned how depraved one human can be to another."

Images crowded his head but this time he didn't ruthlessly push them away. Tightening his grip on her hand he allowed them to float in front of him one by one, hoping that familiarity would eventually take away the pain of remembering.

"They hurt you terribly. I can see it in your expression."

He swallowed hard, his throat tight. "Yes. They weren't shy about using pain to coerce me to talk."

Her hazel eyes were bright with unshed tears. He shouldn't

have told her. She was too soft-hearted, too innocent of the things he'd seen even before he'd been captured. "I'm sorry that happened to you but I'm glad you escaped. I'm glad you're okay."

Steepling his fingers, he rested his elbows on the countertop. "Okay? I'm not sure what that means anymore. I can function day to day and do my job. I don't jump and climb under furniture when I hear gunfire, so that's a positive. I'm not looking over my shoulder paranoid about the world. So I guess you could say I'm okay. There are people walking around a lot more fucked up than I am. Maybe everyone is…in their own way."

"But you can't sleep?"

Jason rubbed his chin and tried to smile. "You're not going to let this go, are you? I can't sleep because it's quiet and dark." He hopped up from the stool to rinse out his cup, not wanting her to see how this subject could still mess with him. "They held me in an underground cell. There was no light except a strip of sun that would come in during the day. At night it was pitch black. And quiet. So fucking quiet. It made the waiting seem like it went on forever."

Those few weeks in that cell had felt like a lifetime. Even when he'd escaped he'd been afraid that it was all a dream. That reality was the prison and freedom was a fantasy that he'd created as he slowly went out of his mind. It was strange how quickly sanity could desert a man when death and pain were his only companions.

Jason needed to shut the hell up but she'd opened the flood-gates with her gentle questions and sympathetic tears. Those tears were trailing down her cheeks, her hand covering her mouth in horror. If he had any fucking sense he'd stop talking and send her to bed.

But he wasn't all that smart. Not about this.

"It got to where I could tell who was coming by the sound of their shoes on the dirt and stones. It was a good thing to know. If it was one of the men coming to take me for interrogation I could prepare myself mentally. Or maybe it was just someone who would walk by my cell to another poor bastard. While I was there I heard them take away three people that never came back."

He'd been waiting for that day. Knowing it would come. The only question was when and how they would finally kill him and put him out of his misery. The electrical shocks. The beatings. Funny how the thing he most remembered was being thirsty. It seemed like he could never get enough water. It explained why he now had a case of bottled water in the refrigerator and another in the pantry. He kept extra bottles in the truck. He never wanted to be caught without it.

"God, Jason." The words seemed torn from Brinley's throat. He was ashamed that he'd said anything. She hadn't done anything to deserve to carry this shit around with her.

He abandoned the cup in the sink and came around the kitchen island, pulling her into his arms, her body trembling with emotion. He was humbled to be with a woman who could feel that deeply for someone other than herself. "Hey, no crying, sweetheart. It's over and done with. The past. I'm alive. That's the only thing that's important."

He brushed at her damp cheeks and she nodded, blinking

away the tears. "I know you haven't told me half of what happened to you."

And he never would. He'd already told her too much. "What happened isn't important. I've learned to live in the present. It's just some nights it's tough, that's all."

"That's when you sit outside and read, isn't it? I've seen you when I couldn't sleep too," she sniffled.

"If I'd known you were awake I would have invited you over for a movie marathon." Jason wanted to lighten the atmosphere that had grown between them. He didn't want her feeling sorry for him. He sure as shit didn't feel sorry for himself. It was his own damn fault he'd been captured.

Jason finally got a smile in return, albeit a tad watery. "Now you know. I'd love to watch movies with you."

Jason looked down at the canine sleeping at his feet. "What do you say, Huck? Should we pop a movie in and see who falls asleep first? My guess it will be the dog."

"I think you're right. What movie should we watch?"

It didn't matter. She'd taken her pill and would be asleep before long. Maybe he could sleep as well with her beside him and the noise of the television in the background.

"Pick anything out you like," he offered, tucking a blanket around her as they settled on the couch. "I'll even watch a chick flick."

She rolled her eyes and chose *Weekend at Bernie's* but the movie had barely begun before her head drooped onto his shoulder, fast asleep. Jason listened to her even breathing as her palm settled on his chest, right over his heart. Like it belonged there.

This woman had wormed her way past all the defenses he'd so carefully erected around him, knocking them over effortlessly. Jason didn't know her well but already she was important to him. She meant something, although he had no clue exactly what. Or even if he was in any shape to find out.

But he liked her.

She made him laugh and she made him think.

When she touched him her fingers felt like flames licking the flesh and made it hard to breathe.

Lust or something else didn't change the mission.

Keep Brinley Snow safe. And alive.

Chapter Ten

BRAD ENRIGHT WAS everything Roger Gaines wasn't. Handsome, fit, tanned, charming, and successful. From the little Brinley knew of Roger it was difficult to imagine the two men being friends. They seemed to have nothing at all in common.

"How long did you know Roger?" Jason asked as they settled into Enright's large and extravagant office. Dressed in an impeccably cut blue suit, expensively styled dark hair, and diamond cuff links, Brad was the epitome of the prosperous businessman. Their research had revealed that the dealership had been in the Enright family since the 1940s with Brad taking the helm a few years ago when his grandfather retired.

Showing off blindingly white teeth, Brad smiled as he unbuttoned his suit jacket and settled into the huge black leather chair. "Since kindergarten. The teacher put us in alphabetical order and there was no one in the class who started with 'F'. The rest is history. Of course I haven't seen much of Roger these last few years. I've been busy here." Brad picked up a glass statuette from his desk and held it up proudly. "We're the number one dealer in luxury automobiles in the state of Montana. Say, what do you drive? You know your vehicle says a lot about who you are. What statement do you want to make, Mr. Anderson?"

"I'll have to give that some thought," Jason answered smoothly when Brinley might have stomped on the man's shiny black shoes. He seemed awfully happy despite losing a close childhood friend. "So you've known Roger since kindergarten but you haven't spent much time together lately. When was the last time you saw him?"

Brad sat back and gazed off into the distance for a moment. "I guess it was about six months ago. My daughter had her second birthday and Roger came to the party."

"Did you notice anything strange?" Brinley found herself asking, only to be on the receiving end of a quelling look from Jason.

Oops. I was supposed to be quiet.

"About Roger?" Brad chuckled and began to play with a couple of paper clips on the desk. "Roger has always been a little strange. Smart but strange. But I guess he was acting weirder than normal. He was pale like he hadn't seen the sun in months. He didn't bring a gift which I thought was kind of rude. Well, at least my wife Trudi thought it was but it didn't surprise me all that much. But the strangest thing was all he could talk about was murder. The guy was obsessed. From what he said he hung around other people just like him. They talked about blood spatter and autopsies. My mother-in-law said she found him gruesome. The way he was that day? I can't say I blame her."

"Was he always like this?" Jason asked, leaning forward. "Had he always fixated on murder?"

"Hell, no," Brad declared, shaking his head. "Roger was a

normal kid. We built forts and played baseball. Ate popsicles and rode bikes. Nothing unusual. Shit, he lettered in three sports in high school. He dated the prom queen and was valedictorian of our graduating class."

That didn't sound like the slacker who lived in filth in his brother's bonus room over the garage.

"When did Roger change?"

Shrugging his shoulders, Brad shifted in his chair. "I'm not sure. In college, I guess. He got more and more involved with life on the Internet. That's where he met his latest girlfriend. He talked about her at the party." Brad tapped his pen on the desk. "What was her name? Let's see… Anita-something. Yes, Anita Hazlitt. He said she lived in a little town near here but I don't remember what it was. She probably knows more about Roger these days than I do."

Jason finished scribbling down the information. "So everything was normal in high school but he changed in college. Are you sure it was college? Did anything traumatic happen in high school? Like did he break up with the prom queen or anything?"

Brad stiffened in his chair, his back ramrod straight. "They broke up right after graduation when Roger visited his grandparents in Florida for the summer."

"Was Roger upset about that?" Jason persisted. "Did he talk about what happened in Florida?"

Brad stood up, clearly indicating that the interview was over. "No, he never did talk about Florida. Now if you will excuse me I do have to get back to work."

As a teacher Brinley was a student of body language, and this guy was lying about the dog eating his homework. It was written all over him. And it had started with breaking up with the prom queen.

She and Jason stood also and she followed him to the door. She was supposed to be quiet and not ask any questions but Jason was already mad at her. One more probably wasn't going to make any difference.

"Whatever happened to the prom queen, Mr. Enright? Does she still live in Billings? Is she still in touch with Roger?"

Enright's lips flattened and he slowly and deliberately buttoned his jacket. "She's my wife Trudi. So I guess you could say they were still in touch."

✦ ✦ ✦

JASON HADN'T SAID a word to Brinley since they'd left the office of Brad Enright and climbed back into the truck. After Enright's admission that Roger had dated his wife years ago, Jason had turned on his heel and sat right back down. He'd peppered the car salesman with several more questions until the man finally admitted that things had been very tense between the two of them all through high school and college.

They were more frenemies than friends – constantly competing and trying to one-up the other guy. But at the end of the interview Enright insisted he didn't have a motive for killing Roger.

Because he'd won. Roger's life sucked and Brad's was a dream come true.

"So will you just yell at me and get it over with? I was supposed to stay quiet and I didn't. I'm sorry."

Jason pulled out into traffic before answering. "I'm not mad."

"You look mad."

A muscle was ticking in his jaw and he hadn't made eye contact for several minutes. In her book that meant he was pissed off.

"I'm not mad," he repeated. "At least not at you. More at myself. I knew he was hiding something but I was going to let him off the hook today and come back another time when he'd had a chance to stew about things."

"And I ruined that."

Jason laughed and finally turned to look at her. "You could have really messed things up. But this time you didn't. You got lucky. We know much more now than we knew before."

Turning into the parking lot of a chain restaurant, Jason put the truck in park. "So you aren't mad?"

"I'm not mad." He shook a finger at her playfully. "But that doesn't mean you have free rein. We might not be so lucky next time."

"There'll be a next time?"

She didn't want to sit at home waiting for him to fill her in. She needed to be a part of this with an urgency that shocked her. After the attempted burglary or whatever it was last night this had become personal.

"I'm not letting you out of my sight so you're stuck with me. Now let's go have something to eat and call West. He should have the autopsy results by now. Then we'll call Jared and have him find out about Trudi and this love triangle."

That sounded like a good plan. She hadn't eaten much this

morning, still upset about someone breaking into her home. "What about Anita Hazlitt?"

Jason chuckled and reached under his seat, pulling out a tablet computer. "Let's hope she doesn't have an unlisted number."

"And if she does?"

"That only means it won't be easy. Are you ready to go inside?"

She was ready to get some answers. It was beginning to feel like the more they learned the less they knew.

Chapter Eleven

ANITA HAZLITT WASN'T going to be easy to find. A quick Google search didn't turn anything up, but then they didn't know her address or even the town she lived in. Jason needed to call Jared about doing a quick search for the woman. Unless she was deliberately hiding it wouldn't take long to locate her.

Back in Tremont Jason was sitting at his kitchen table with a beer and a stack of mail that he'd neglected for too long. It was going to be another long night. He could already tell. With the television on and Brinley beside him on the couch he'd managed a decent amount of sleep. He doubted he would be so lucky again this evening. He was wide awake, his mind working on the puzzle of Roger Gaines. So far Brad Enright seemed the most logical suspect but it was still early in the investigation.

Brinley joined him in the kitchen, snagging the last root beer from the refrigerator. "Fran and Richard are sitting on their deck. I'm going to go say hello. I don't remember if I even thanked them last night so I should probably do that too."

She was spending the night with Jason again. She'd been disappointed when they'd driven up and her front door was still plywood. There had been a note on the porch that the handyman had to order a new one and it might be in tomorrow. Jason didn't bother telling her that he probably would have made her stay in his home anyway. Somehow she was the key to this mystery and until he figured out why he planned to keep a close eye on her.

"If you wait a minute I'll go with you."

"I'll be fine." She put her hands on her hips and gave him a disgusted look. "I'm going two houses down. I'll be within shouting distance. Do I have to be babysat every single minute?"

No, he simply liked her company.

"It's fine if you want to talk to them. I have a phone call to make and then I'll come down and join you."

Visibly relaxed, she practically skipped out of the front door with glee, apparently fed up with only Jason for company. With a room full of kids all day long she probably needed more extrovert time than he did. As much as he liked socializing with people it also mentally exhausted him. He needed alone time to recharge his batteries.

Pulling out his cell phone, Jason punched in a few buttons and waited for West to answer.

"It's about time you called me. I've been waiting to hear from you."

And West gave Jason shit about how he answered the phone...

"It's nice to talk to you too, bro. I've got information for you. What do you have to tell me?"

Jason heard West snapping at someone, his tone short and impatient. Whatever West had to say wasn't good news. He would have made a terrible poker player.

"Roger Gaines died from a gunshot wound to the heart. Thirty-eight caliber. Coroner confirmed death to be around eight at night."

"Nothing we didn't know," Jason observed. "Is that it?"

"Pretty much. Roger Gaines was in mediocre health for a man so young. His weight was too high, his muscle tone terrible, and his arteries already showed the effects of a junk food diet paired with a sedentary lifestyle. Add twenty years to his age and he would have been a ticking time bomb."

Those facts went along with what they'd found out from Stuart Gaines. Jason quickly filled West in on what he'd learned today.

"What about forensics?"

"I don't have it all back yet but I can tell you that you were right about one thing. The standard is for every room to have six plastic cups on the counter."

"So he did have company. The killer was someone he knew."

"Or he could have used the cups earlier and threw them away," West pointed out. "It gives credence to your theory but it doesn't prove it. I will concede that I agree that the killer was someone he wasn't afraid of. He didn't fight or struggle. As for finding any trash from the room in nearby dumpsters? We came up empty."

Jason growled in frustration. "This guy isn't stupid. I feel like he knew what he was doing. He planned it out. This was no spur of the moment thing."

"But why would someone plot to kill some guy who is basically a nerd. The most dangerous thing Gaines did was read about murder from the safety of his brother's home. That's not going to get you killed generally."

"What about fingerprints?" Jason doubted the killer had been that careless. He seemed to have covered all the bases.

"We got a couple of hits in the database but I was able to weed them from the suspect list. They both had solid alibis. One's in jail and the other was at work a hundred miles away with about a dozen witnesses."

Shit and double shit.

"So basically we got nothing. That's great. I'm going to have Jared check out Brad Enright. He was supposedly Roger's best friend from kindergarten but he admitted today that they competed with each other."

"Nothing wrong with a little healthy competition. That hardly makes him a suspect," West observed.

"It does if Enright married Roger's high school sweetheart," Jason laughed, remembering the car salesman's expression when he'd revealed that little detail. "In my book that makes a possible motive."

"So maybe Stuart Gaines killed his little brother because he was a huge sponge, living off Stuart's hard work. Or perhaps Brad Enright killed him because of some jealousy thing. I've got to tell you it's not much to go on."

It wasn't and that bugged the hell out of Jason. How could one man have so little contact with the outside world and still be physically alive? Somewhere there was a person who interacted with Gaines regularly – maybe even on a daily basis.

"Enright told us about a new girlfriend. She's unlisted so I'll have Jared take a run at finding her. Hopefully he can do that overnight so I can talk to her tomorrow."

West sighed. "I'd love to shake loose from this case and go with you. Anything to get me away from the mayor. He called me six times today."

Jason's brother was working on the ritual-like murder of a teenager. Murders of kids trumped adults every time and this one was taking all of West's attention, which was fine with Jason. He didn't need a babysitter to do his job.

"About what?"

"Hell if I know," West retorted, dislike in his tone. "To bitch, mostly. Election time can't come too soon."

"You could end up with someone much worse," Jason warned with a laugh. "Maybe you should think about running yourself. The Andersons have friends in this town. You'd probably get some support."

There was muffled choking on the other end of the call which told Jason loud and clear what his brother thought of the idea of running for office. Or using his family connections.

"Never say that out loud again. I mean never."

"Then I better hang up because I can't think of any other way to solve your problem. I'll call you in the morning."

Jason rang off and then quickly dialed Jared, hoping he wouldn't wake the baby, Elizabeth Rose. Jared picked up on the first ring.

"Did I wake her?" Jason asked, taking a swig from his beer bottle.

"She's asleep and so is Misty. Let me get into the den so I won't bother her." Jason heard the sound of a door and then another. "Okay, we can talk. I've got information for you. Really interesting stuff."

This was the first good news of the day.

"I'm listening." Jason slid the pen and notebook in front of him and paged to an empty space. "Go ahead."

"You asked me to investigate your neighbor Brinley Snow and I did find out a few things. She had a restraining order against some guy – Tom Leeds – back in Chicago. From what I can tell he was the father of one of her students. Apparently Brinley felt the little girl should be held back a year and the father lost his ever-loving mind. Started following her around. Showing up at restaurants and movies. Sitting in front of her apartment. She received threatening letters and Leeds even tried to get her fired. Told the school board she was hitting and verbally abusing the kids in her class. It was a fucking mess."

"Let me guess. They had to investigate her because of the allegations."

Anger churned in Jason's gut at the unjustness of Brinley's situation. Anyone who had spent five minutes with the woman would know she wouldn't hurt or abuse someone.

"It gets better. Leeds was a big shot in the Windy City and had a couple of board members in his pocket to make her life extra special horrible. Eventually the whole case fell apart when several influential parents came to her defense but it was a real cluster for awhile. Brinley resigned and took a year off tutoring at one of those centers for gifted children. I'm not sure how she heard about the opening in Tremont but she was hired and moved here in April."

And moved in next door the first week of May. Only days after Mrs. Barnes had moved out and into an assisted living facility.

"Maybe Leeds isn't over the whole thing, although how he would know Roger Gaines I have no idea. You didn't find a connection?"

"None," Jared said flatly. "And believe me, I looked. If they've ever had any contact they've hidden it well. I'd make sure you protect Ms. Snow. If Leeds is out there and still upset, he might escalate from stalking to something more up close and personal."

Which reminded him that Brinley was out of his sight. After hearing this he couldn't let that happen.

"Where was Leeds at the time of death?"

"A birthday party for his daughter. Plenty of witnesses but he's rich enough to hire people."

"It's a stretch," Jason admitted. "It's doubtful Leeds would go off after all this time."

"I'm not done researching him. If there's something there I'll find it," Jared vowed. "Which reminds me, I'll have more information for you on Roger Gaines by morning. I've got a program running right now."

"Add one more. Anita Hazlitt." Jason spelled her name and gave the few particulars that he had. "I want to talk to her. Preferably tomorrow. If you don't have time I can do it."

"Then let me get back to work. If I have any issues I'll send you a text by midnight. You'll be awake?"

"Aren't I always?" Jason couldn't keep the sarcasm out of his tone but Jared wasn't a man to take offense easily. "Seriously, I'll be up. Tonight's going to be one of those nights."

"Then I'll report back. Talk to you later."

Jared hung up, leaving Jason pondering everything he'd

learned. Perhaps it was time for him and Brinley to have a heart to heart talk.

Just how many secrets did his pretty neighbor have?

✦ ✦ ✦

IT WAS ANOTHER gorgeous summer night and Brinley should have been relaxed, enjoying the cooler evening temperatures. But she couldn't stop thinking about the break in and the thought of someone pawing through her belongings. She'd walked through this morning and nothing looked missing. Richard had probably scared off the burglar before he'd had a chance to steal anything but it was still unnerving.

She'd moved here for a fresh start. A new home.

She'd wanted to feel safe and now she felt anything but.

"Are you sure you don't want a glass of wine? It might help you sleep."

Fran held up the bottle of Chardonnay but Brinley shook her head. She wasn't a huge fan of alcohol and with the wheels turning in her brain a mile a minute even a whole bottle of wine wasn't going to make her sleepy. She was wide awake.

"No, thank you. I really just came over here to thank you both for everything. For scaring away the intruder and then meeting the repairman today. I feel so lucky to have such great neighbors."

Jason, too, but she didn't mention him. Her personal feelings for the handsome man were all mixed up with the drama of murder. She was attracted to him but it was more than that. When she was with him she felt safe.

And after everything she'd been through she knew how special that was.

"Will you be gone tomorrow too?" Fran asked, settling back on the lounge chair with a contented sigh. "I can let the repairman in again."

When Brinley had become friends with Fran and Richard she'd given them a spare key and they'd happily given her one of theirs. She'd let in the pest control man for the couple just a few weeks ago.

"I'm not sure what Jason has planned but if you could I would be very grateful. It's such an eyesore right now."

"You should have seen our kitchen when we remodeled. Complete and total devastation. We ate out for months." Richard laughed and refilled his glass, nodding toward her driveway. "Looks like you have company."

Brinley wouldn't have used such a polite word.

Greg was hopping out of his car and striding up her front porch steps, not seeing her on the deck between the houses. For a moment she pondered letting him bang on the door while she hid in Fran and Richard's house but that was the coward's way. She needed to deal with Greg once and for all.

The relationship wasn't going to go anywhere. She hadn't given him a thought last night or all day. If she were being brutally honest, he had nothing on Jason Anderson. It wasn't even a competition.

"I'll go talk to him. I'll be right back."

It wouldn't take long. She wasn't planning on dragging this out. She met him at the bottom of her porch steps as he turned to leave.

"Greg, I didn't know you were coming over."

Because you didn't call. Again. Asshole.

Greg was apparently the type that thought women were sitting around twiddling their thumbs until a man called or showed up. He must have been pissed about her absence because she'd heard him pound on the front door as if he owned the joint. Her creep detector was going off big time. She needed to cut this guy loose for good.

His thunderous expression instantly changed to a charming smile. "Brinley, I thought you weren't home. I was hoping we might have a glass of wine together." Greg held up a bottle. "But now I'm just worried about you. What happened to your door?"

"Someone broke in. They kicked in my door so I'm waiting for a new one." Brinley took a deep breath. She hated this part of dating. "Listen, Greg, you're a nice guy and all but I just don't think this is going to work out between us. I hope we can be friends."

Or not. Whatever. Don't feel obligated to stay in touch. I won't.

He stiffened and his smile fell. "I thought things were going really well. We've had fun."

"This just isn't a good time in my life for a relationship." Next century wasn't looking too good either. "I just think our dating wouldn't be productive."

That charming smile was back. "I bet I could change your mind. Let's go inside and have a glass of wine. Talk about things."

He didn't listen well. In fact, she had second graders who had better listening skills.

"First of all, my house is a crime scene," she countered, just wanting him to leave. "Second, I don't want to have a glass of wine. I don't want to talk."

She didn't bother to hide the edge to her tone that said she was annoyed. He didn't seem to get subtlety but she didn't want to have to hit him over the head with a brick. Figuratively only, of course.

"Brinley, Richard was thinking of building a bonfire and roasting some marshmallows." Fran rounded the corner of the house. "Would you be interested? I think I have chocolate and graham crackers to make s'mores. They're my favorite."

Saved by the neighbor.

"That sounds delicious, Fran. I'll be right there."

Greg frowned at the intrusion but seemed to decide that retreat was the best option. "I'm sorry you feel that way. I guess I'll just leave."

Bottle hugged to his midsection, he whirled on his heel and stomped back to his car, gunning the engine as he sped down the road. Jason had come outside to join them and he watched Greg's taillights disappear into the night.

"Who was that?"

"Greg. I don't think he'll be back."

"Why was he here in the first place?"

Fran laughed and linked her arm with Brinley's. "I think he's an admirer. Persistent fellow too. Let's go have marshmallows."

"Actually–" Jason began and then paused. "Fran, would you mind if we took a raincheck on marshmallows? I need Brinley for something."

For something? Way to be vague. Hopefully it had something to do with Roger Gaines.

"Of course we can." Fran waved away his concern. "You two go have fun."

Fran was waggling her eyebrows as Jason marched toward his own house and Brinley wanted to groan in embarrassment. It was clear her neighbor thought that something more than…well…simple neighborliness was going on in Jason's house. This was going to be all over town by noon tomorrow.

Brinley caught up to Jason and grabbed his arm. "She thinks we're going to…you know. She thinks we're a couple."

"Fran loves good gossip. Even if you and I were snarking at each other she'd think that." He picked up her hand and a tingle ran up her arm. "I don't know about you but I doubt I can sleep tonight. So I was thinking we could go for a night ride at the ranch. Can you ride a horse?"

It was dangerous to her equilibrium to be alone with a man as fine as Jason Anderson but she couldn't think of one good reason not to go. If she were honest she wanted to. Last night she'd felt so close to him.

She wanted to feel that way again.

"I've ridden a few times at summer camp. I wouldn't say I was good at it but I can probably hold on."

"I'll get you a gentle mount. Let's go." Jason patted his pocket and then pulled out car keys. "Thanks for coming with me."

At this moment, she'd follow wherever he led her.

Chapter Twelve

JASON HAD CHOSEN a gentle horse for Brinley and had saddled his own stallion Rebel for himself. The steady rhythm of the hooves as they ambled along the path lulled them into a sense of quiet contentment that Jason was loath to break.

"I can't believe how many stars I can see here in Montana," Brinley breathed, her head tipped back to take in the purple night sky. "We didn't have anything like this in Chicago."

She'd handed him the perfect opening on a silver platter. He hated to ruin the serenity between them but he had questions he needed answered if they were ever going to get to the bottom of this case.

"I'd like to hear more about Chicago. There's a little spot not far away next to a pretty stream. We can sit and talk."

"That sounds good. I need to stretch my legs or I'm going to be really sore tomorrow."

She'd told him she hadn't ridden in about fifteen years so she was going to be sore tomorrow no matter what, but stretching her muscles wasn't a bad idea. When they arrived at the clearing near the stream Jason nose tied the horses and led her to an old fallen log where they could sit. He should have brought some wine or something to help relax her.

"So tell me about Chicago," he opened, deliberately keeping the question vague.

"I told you about my family. What else do you want to know?"

Her tone was light but Jason sensed an uneasiness in the way she held her body stiffly next to his. She didn't want to talk about this.

"What made you move to Tremont?"

He couldn't see her face well in the moonlight but he could tell she wasn't smiling or laughing. "A new job. I wanted a fresh start. A place where I wasn't the middle sister in the Snow family. I can be whatever I want here."

"What do you want to be?"

"Happy," she answered simply, still looking at the stars. "I want to be happy."

"You weren't happy in Chicago?"

"I was as happy as I could be but I couldn't shake the feeling that there was something more out there."

He steeled himself for her reaction. "Did the Tom Leeds situation make you unhappy?'

Jason heard the quick intake of her breath just before she hopped to her feet. He'd hit a nerve.

"I see you've been doing your homework. Is that what you were doing while I slept last night or did you have your brother do your dirty work?"

Brinley hadn't bothered to disguise the disdain in her tone and he couldn't really blame her. He was a man that liked his privacy and wouldn't enjoy being investigated any more than she did.

"Actually I had one of my partners, Jared Monroe, do the research. Are you surprised that I had to do it? I needed to see if you had some link to Roger Gaines."

She spun around, her body rigid with anger. "I told you I didn't. You don't believe me, obviously."

He could hear the hurt in her voice and felt about one inch tall knowing he had put it there. He needed to make her understand this was about the case and not about her. He believed in her and everything she said.

Jason stood as well but she backed away, clearly not wanting to be near him. "I do believe you. But there might have been something you weren't even aware of. How can I ask you tell me something that you don't know?"

"Tom Leeds doesn't have anything to do with this. You were just poking around in my life looking for some kind of scandal. Well, you found one. I wonder what I'd find if I did the same to you."

More than she'd bargained for, that was for sure.

"I wasn't," he tried again. "If you're the one clue to a murder I'd be a lousy damn cop not to check into your past. Let me ask you this…what would you say if I asked you to tell me about your life?"

"I don't know," she shrugged, crossing her arms over her chest. "I was born in Chicago. My life has been pretty uneventful. I went to the University of Illinois and became an elementary school teacher in a private school. I'm not married and I don't have any kids."

"I hope you can see how that wouldn't help me in the least. I didn't want to upset you but I guess I should have told you straight out that I was delving into your background. I apologize."

Brinley's chin lifted and then she nodded. "Thank you. And I do understand. I really do. I was just upset that you mentioned Tom Leeds. That's a situation I thought I had left far behind me."

Glad that they were back on friendly terms, Jason reached and took her hand in his, gratified when she didn't pull away. He didn't want them to be enemies. If the arousal stirring inside him at the touch of her skin was any indication, he wanted something much more.

"Will you tell me about it? Is he still an issue?"

If this guy was making life difficult for Brinley Jason would happily get involved. Holding himself very still, he waited while she decided if she could trust him. Even in the moonlight he could watch the expressions flit across her features one by one until she settled on acceptance.

"No, he's not a problem any longer. He really wasn't even before I left Chicago." Still holding his hand, she tugged him back to the fallen log where they'd been sitting earlier. "I think I better start at the beginning."

Jason settled next to her while she gathered her thoughts. He wished he didn't have to make her talk about something that was obviously upsetting but he didn't have a choice. It was the life in law enforcement... Weeding through good people to find the bad. Sometimes innocents could get hurt in the process.

"I met Tom when I was teaching his daughter. He came to a parent-teacher conference and he was—oh, I don't know—

charming, I guess. Very charismatic. He had money and connections and he swept me off my feet. I kept saying that we couldn't date and that it wouldn't be ethical but he continued to send flowers and gifts. He wouldn't take no for an answer."

A million warning bells went off in Jason's brain all at once hearing her describe some rich douchebag who pouted when he didn't get what he wanted. Brinley seemed too down to earth to fall for a guy like that.

"So I finally went out on a couple of dates with him." She groaned and rested her head in her hands for a moment. "To say that he and I weren't compatible is an understatement. He wanted someone to listen to him. Adore him. Needless to say after two dates I told him I didn't think things were going to work out between us. That's when the trouble started."

"Sounds like he needed an attitude adjustment," Jason observed, ready and willing to give the lesson if need be. "So he started stalking you."

"Not right away. At first it was more subtle. He spread rumors about me at the school. Made it difficult to work there. Then he went to the board and said I wanted to keep his daughter Cicely back for second grade. It wasn't even true. Cicely had issues but academics weren't one of them. Mostly she wanted attention from her father and she didn't care much how she got it. She was a real behavioral problem."

"And the board listened to him," Jason prompted. "Sided with him?"

Brinley rubbed her temple and nodded. "Some of them did, yes. I didn't find out until later but several of the board members knew what he was like. He'd done this before to another teacher a few years ago. God knows who he's torturing now."

She shuddered delicately and he didn't hesitate to place an arm around her, pulling her close to him. Resting her head on his shoulder, he felt her relax against him. Humbled by her forgiveness and trust, he stroked her hair and let her finish the story at her own pace.

"Even when it was over and he'd moved on to another victim I knew I needed a change. I quit and took another job but it wasn't what I was looking for. I have a teacher friend who works in Denver who has a friend in Tremont. My family was shocked when I accepted the job but I have no regrets. This was the new start I'd been looking for and not just because of Tom Leeds." She looked up at him and his heart skipped a beat at her beautiful face outlined in the moonlight. "I never mentioned Tom because I don't think it could be him. He's moved on and so have I."

"He has an alibi and Jared can't find a connection to Roger Gaines."

"Because there isn't one. Tom Leeds is a dead end."

Jason hoped that was the case. "I just need to make sure. I can't be too careful with your safety."

"You worry a lot. I'm fine. No one is going to mess with me with you around to scare them off."

"That was the plan. But what about that guy tonight? Do I need to scare him off too?"

Jason hadn't yet met the idiot who had cancelled dinner on Brinley the other night and had only seen him drive away earlier this evening but he would happily let the guy know that he was no longer in the running.

Brinley deserved better.

"Greg? I don't think I'll be seeing him again. I told him that it wasn't going to work out."

"How did he take it?"

"He wasn't happy but I think he got the message. There wasn't really anything between us. We'd only been out a few times. I met him at the coffee shop. We didn't even kiss."

Confirmation this Greg guy wasn't very bright. "Two dates and he didn't kiss you? He's a slow mover."

"Maybe he wasn't that attracted to me. What do you usually do by the second date?" Brinley slapped her hand over her mouth and giggled. "Forget I asked that. I'm not sure I want to know."

"Of course he was attracted to you. Who wouldn't be? I sure as hell wouldn't be just holding hands with a beautiful and desirable woman. I'd at the very least get a kiss on the first date."

✦ ✦ ✦

THE ELECTRICITY HAD been building between Brinley and Jason for the last twenty-four hours. Maybe more. When she'd fallen asleep in his arms last night, she'd never felt more safe and protected despite the fact that she might be in danger. She trusted that Jason would never let anything happen to her.

Now hearing that he found her attractive…even beautiful and desirable made her heart leap at his softly spoken words. Gathering every bit of courage she had inside she gazed into his eyes, curiosity winning over fear.

"Is this our first date?" she asked, trying to sound light and playful but her throat was tight with an unnamed emotion. Arousal swirled in her belly whenever Jason was near. She needed to know if he felt the same.

Jason smiled, a dimple appearing in his cheek. "The night you invited me to dinner was our first date. And then last night when we watched movies together was probably our second. So this would be number three."

Brinley had a decent idea of what Jason did with a woman on the third date and she wasn't nearly ready for that. He was a good man and she was attracted to him but she'd been burned before, moving too fast in a relationship.

One step at a time.

"I don't think those count but we can call this our first date."

She tried to keep her tone neutral but the words came out rushed and breathless. Wiping her damp palms on her shorts, she tried to rein in her racing heart. The thought of kissing Jason overwhelmed everything and anything.

His hand slid behind her neck and tugged her closer, heat sweeping through her from head to toe. "Then we both know what comes next."

His hands stroked up and down her spine in a slow, soothing motion that did little to settle the maelstrom of emotions whirling inside. Her bones turned to jelly under his hypnotic ministrations even as her breath hitched at his touch.

She let her hands slide up his strong arms, feeling the hard muscle under her palms. His skin felt warm as her fingers trailed up his shoulders to loop around his neck. He had moved closer, and his lips were mere inches from her own. She could feel his warm breath as his lips slowly descended. He stopped mere millimeters from kissing her.

"I've wanted to do this since the first day I saw you."

Then his lips were on hers. The kiss began as a gentle whisper, a brush of his mouth. She'd expected an alpha male such as Jason to devour and dominate but instead he seduced and cajoled, drawing her ever closer. Moth to flame. Magnet to pure steel.

Jason nipped at her lower lip and ran his tongue along the seam until she was practically begging him to dip his tongue inside her mouth. His mouth finally sealed with hers and his tongue began a gentle exploration. The sensuous foray sent desire coursing through her veins and settled low in her abdomen. She pressed closer to his body and answered his tongue with her own. Her head spun and her arousal inched higher as she breathed in his delicious scent. Spicy and distinctly male, Brinley let it wash over her, pulling her further from the horrors of the last two days until they were only people in the world.

In his strong arms there was no room for fear, the only danger to her heart.

By the time he dragged his lips from hers everything had changed. They'd moved from casual neighbors to friends to near-lovers in a short forty-eight hours. As much as her body yearned for what she knew would be out of this world pleasure with Jason, her head wouldn't allow total surrender. Some shred of self-preservation held her back from giving him everything.

It was too soon. Too fast. Brinley needed to catch her breath.

She placed her palms on his chest and could feel his heart under her fingers, racing as quickly as her own.

"That was...amazing," she finally said.

"Why do I get the feeling you're not happy about that? Usually an amazing kiss is a good thing."

"It is good," she protested, trying to find the right words to explain what barely made sense in her own mind. "I just don't want to move too fast, that's all. I've done it before and it didn't turn out all that well."

For his part, Jason didn't look too upset by her edict. "I can understand that and respect it. I've done the same. I guess it wouldn't be bad to slow things down, especially since I'm supposed to be keeping you safe, not stripping you naked."

Heat burned in her cheeks as a vision of the two of them undressed and writhing on a bed flashed in front of her eyes. She'd never been much for sex in the past – she usually ended up disappointed – but with Jason it promised to be very good indeed.

"So we'll slow things down then?"

He'd agreed so she couldn't understand why she felt depressed at the mere thought. It was just that the kiss had been so damn hot...

"Slow and steady. That's what I always say."

A take charge kind of man like Jason had probably never said those words in his entire life.

"Really? I haven't heard you say that since I've met you."

Rubbing the back of his neck, Jason gave her a grim smile. "Actually I never say that. I was just trying to be a good sport about getting slapped down."

"You didn't get slapped down. I just..." Brinley took a deep breath and tried to explain. "With everything going on I feel kind of overwhelmed at the moment. It's not that I'm not attracted to you. Because I am–"

"Brinley, stop," Jason commanded, bringing a halt to her emotional babbling. "You don't have to explain anything to me. I get it. You have a lot going on in your life right now and it's okay. I'm not going anywhere. When the time is right we'll both know it. And honestly? This isn't the moment. But when it's time I do have one request."

He was grinning now and she couldn't do anything but smile in return. He'd taken an awkward situation and turned it completely around. Another reason she liked him so much. "Name it."

He leaned closer so he was whispering in her ear. "Be gentle with me."

Choking with laughter, she sighed dramatically and tapped her chin in consideration. "I'm not sure I can promise that."

To her delight Jason chuckled and dropped a kiss on her nose. "Fair enough. How about we head back to the barn?"

Jason helped her mount up and they rode slowly back, taking their time and enjoying the quiet of the evening. He was a special man not to have taken offense. She'd known plenty of males that would have pouted or been angry. He really did understand her need to slow things down.

The funny thing was…now that he'd agreed to do it, she wasn't so damn sure that's what she wanted.

Because she wanted him more than anything.

Chapter Thirteen

THE NEXT MORNING Jason peeked in on a sleeping Brinley before getting to work. Lying with her cheek pillowed on her hand, she looked peaceful and worry free. Not at all like the woman of last night who had been first angry with him for investigating her background and then obviously scared of the two of them moving too fast.

He had pushed too much but the fire that burned between them was too hot to ignore. One way or another, he was going to end up in bed with the pretty Miss Snow. It was only a matter of when, not if.

A knock on the door and Huck barking had Jason jogging down the hall to answer it before Brinley woke up. They'd both stayed up until about two in the morning and he wanted her to get some rest. He was used to not sleeping so it didn't bother him as much.

"You're late," Jason said as he opened the door to his business partner and best friend Logan Wright. Logan had been a small town sheriff when Jason had met him but now he was a full-fledged partner in JLJ Consulting, doing most of the field work. Today he was going to watch over Brinley while Jason and

West went to talk to Anita Hazlitt. "But I'll forgive you if you have donuts."

Logan, with his patented grin, held up a white paper bag even as he scratched Huck behind the ears. "Would I disappoint you? Now get out of my way. I need a cup of coffee stat."

Jason stepped back to allow Logan to pass. "I just made a fresh pot. Help yourself."

Dropping the bag on the counter, Logan reached into the cabinet and pulled down a mug, Huck right beside him.

"So all you need me to do today is a babysitting job? Sounds too easy. There must be a catch or something."

Jason bit into the glazed cruller with relish before tossing a piece to Huck, who downed it in one gulp. "No catch. West and I are going to talk to Roger Gaines's supposed girlfriend and I don't want to take Brinley along. For all we know Anita is the killer. A crime of passion, so to speak. I don't want Brinley in the line of fire if things go south."

"So Jared found her? That man needs to sleep more."

Logan was the father of twin toddlers so he didn't have much room to talk.

"The way you're slurping down that java it looks like you could do with a little more shut eye too."

Logan grinned over his coffee cup. "I do okay in that department. But on those rare occasions both kids are actually asleep, Ava and I have much better things to do than rest."

"I'm a poor, lonely bachelor so spare me the details." Jason held up his sticky hands in surrender.

"With a pretty houseguest to protect you don't sound too lonely to me," Logan shot back with a laugh. "Be careful or you'll end up like the rest of us. Married with kids and driving a minivan."

"Don't give me that shit. You love being a family man. And you don't drive a minivan. You drive a truck."

"By the grace of God," Logan said dramatically. "But didn't Jared tell you? He bought Misty a minivan last week. It's only a matter of time before it becomes the default transportation for them. Poor bastard."

"There are worse things," Jason chuckled at the look of dismay on his friend's face. "Although none come to mind at the moment."

Logan leaned forward as if to say something very private. "Don't tell anyone this…but the other day I was watching something on television. I don't remember what it was. But a commercial for a minivan came on and I actually found myself thinking that it looked like a nice vehicle. Holy shit. Luckily I caught myself in time and told Ava to slap the crap out of me if I ever say the 'M' word. Of course she said she'd be happy to."

"Your secret is safe with me. I'd hate to ruin your reputation as a pain in the ass alpha male stud." Jason popped the last bite of donut into his mouth, the sugar rush just what he'd needed this morning to get going. "I told Brinley before she fell asleep that I was going to have my partner stay with her today so she won't be shocked when she wakes up and I'm gone. Since we don't know if she's in danger don't let her out of your sight. She may not like it but until we know more she's going to have to deal with it."

After refilling his cup Logan sat down at the island and rummaged through the bag for a chocolate frosted. "What is your gut telling you?"

Logan was an instinctual lawman, eschewing rules, regulations, and often evidence that pointed in a certain direction. He trusted the little voice inside of him more than anything.

"You sound like West. The thing is I'm not sure my gut can be trusted. It almost got me killed," Jason admitted. He'd been following his instincts when he was captured by the drug cartel.

"You told me the story but I'm not sure I believe it. Your gut was telling you where the bad guys were. It was just shit luck you were captured. You saved some lives that day."

"My gut is telling me there's a lot more than we know about this case. We haven't found the true motive."

"Generally people kill for one of a few reasons." Logan began ticking them off on his fingers. "Love. Money. Revenge. Anger. Maybe self-defense. Which one are you leaning toward?"

"None of them. That's why this case pisses me off." Jason slapped down his coffee cup in frustration. "Did the brother kill Gaines because of money? Did Enright kill for revenge? I don't think it's self-defense or anger as there were no signs of a struggle. That leaves love. And that's why you're watching Brinley today. Just in case Anita Hazlitt murdered Roger Gaines in a love gone wrong scenario."

"Personally I like this Enright guy for it, but then I'm not following the case very closely. I only know what you've told me."

"Right now he's number one on my list as well." Jason heaved a sigh and rinsed out his cup in the sink. "Jared is checking the man's finances and West – in between all the other shit he has to do – has been looking into how happy that marriage is. Hopefully he'll know something today."

Logan pointed out of the front window. "Speak of the devil. He's pulling into your driveway."

Jason was in a hurry to get to Anita Hazlitt, who lived about an hour out of Tremont in Harper. Seth Reilly was the sheriff there so if there was any trouble, Jason knew that backup wouldn't be far away.

"Take care of Brinley. And Huck." Jason gave the dog a pat on the head. "I should be home before dinner."

Logan popped a piece of donut into his mouth. "Jesus, will you just go find a killer? For someone that's just supposed to be your neighbor you've got your tighty whities in a bunch. Huck and I will take very good care of your lady friend."

Of course Logan would, but now that Jason was heading out the door he was finding that he didn't want to leave Brinley behind.

He was going to miss her today. And that was ten different kinds of messed up. He shouldn't be so attached to her this quickly.

But then last night's kiss hadn't been your regular garden variety first date kiss either. It had been so hot it about singed his eyebrows. Brinley Snow might look innocent, but she sure as hell didn't kiss like one.

"See that you do," Jason growled as he headed out the door to join his brother in the SUV. "And tell Brinley I'll call her later."

"Why bother? I can just pass her a note before study hall. Do you like Jason? Check yes or no."

Jason slammed the door but could still hear Logan's peals of laughter as he descended the porch steps. When he returned tonight he needed to remember to punch Logan right in that gut that he trusted so much.

Chapter Fourteen

"THIS IS IT," West said as he pulled into the apartment complex parking area. "I hope she's home."

"According to Jared she works at night as a waitress so the best chance we have of talking to her is during the day. What I hope is that she actually knows something about this case. Who might want Roger Gaines dead and why?"

"I wish I were that optimistic, brother, but this job has made me cynical as hell."

Jason climbed out of the SUV and looked at the building in front of him. Made of red brick with white trim, it looked like every other apartment building around with floors of doors lined up one by one. Anita Hazlitt lived on the third floor.

"Does that look like what I think it is?" West pointed to a door on the third floor as they approached the stairs. "What was the apartment number again?"

"303," Jason replied grimly, taking the stairs two at a time. It looked like they were too fucking late. Yellow crime scene tape crisscrossed the apartment door.

"Fuck," West hissed under his breath as they stood in front of the taped off entrance. "This is not good. Not good at all."

"We'll go see Seth. Hopefully Anita Hazlitt is okay."

"I got a bad feeling about this. It's too much of a coincidence."

"What are you doing here? What do you want?" a feminine voice from behind them asked.

Jason whirled around and must have scared the young woman because her face turned pale and she practically fell over her own feet stepping back. West caught her arm and kept her from sprawling on the concrete. Tall and slender with short dark hair, she appeared to be in her early twenties.

"Easy there." West patted the woman on the shoulder and then reached for his badge. "We're the good guys. I'm Westin Anderson, Head of Detectives in Tremont and this is my brother Jason. We're sorry if we scared you."

The girls seemed to relax slightly but she still clutched her purse to her chest like a shield. She peered at West's badge and then nodded. "Why are the cops from Tremont here? Sheriff Reilly said he was releasing the apartment to me this morning."

Clearly they needed to talk to Seth and find out what had happened here.

Jason hooked his thumb at the door. "You live here? With Anita Hazlitt? We need to talk to her. Are you a friend?"

"I'm her roommate. Lita George."

Her gaze darted back and forth between Jason and West as if she expected them to do something evil or violent. Jason held out his hand and gave her his best non-threatening smile.

"It's nice to meet you, Lita. Do you know when Anita will be home? We really need to talk to her."

"Is this about one of her cases? I always knew that she was

going to get in trouble one day and I was right."

Cases?

"Actually this is about her boyfriend Roger Gaines." Jason watched for any change in Lita's expression when he mentioned their victim's name.

Lita rolled her eyes. "Did Roger tell you Anita was his girlfriend? She'll get a big kick out of that. They were friends but she thought he was pretty geeky. Everyone did."

"When you say cases, Lita, what did you mean by that?" West asked, giving Jason a sidelong glance. "What kind of trouble is Anita in?"

"You really don't know, do you?" Lita tilted her head in question and tears welled up in her eyes. "Someone shot Anita yesterday evening while she was walking home from a friend's place. I knew this was going to happen. She took too many chances and now look what's happened."

Full-fledged tears were running down Lita's face and although Jason had a million questions for this young woman, the first thing he needed to do was comfort the poor thing. She'd obviously been through a great deal if what she said was true.

"How about we go inside and sit down? West will make you some tea," Jason offered. "Seth said he was releasing the apartment? They searched it for clues?"

"Yes, he called me this morning and said I could come back and get my things. I don't want to sleep here alone." Lita shuddered but reached into her purse and pulled out a set of keys. "I'm going to move in with my parents until they catch whoever did this."

They followed Lita into the apartment and sat down on the

couch but Jason's fingers were flying over his cell phone, texting Seth to find out how serious the injuries were and if they had any suspects. West took off his cowboy hat and set it on the side table while Lita settled on a chair to Jason's right.

"If you point me in the right direction I'll fix that tea for you, ma'am," West offered.

Lita scrubbed at her cheeks and shook her head. "I don't really need it but I guess I should be offering you something since you're the guest. I think we have some sodas in the refrigerator."

Jason shook his head, sympathy welling up inside him for this young woman. She'd been through the wringer and when he told her about Roger it was only going to get worse. He needed to be as gentle in his questioning as possible.

"We don't need anything. I'd like to hear about what happened to Anita and why you thought it might have something to do with her cases. Can you tell me about that?"

Lita's fingers plucked at the upholstery on the chair arm. "I think a murderer that she was investigating shot her because she was getting too close to the truth. You see, Anita likes to investigate unsolved cases. You know…murders and missing people. That's how she met Roger. They were both in some online group and found out they lived pretty close to one another. They'd meet up about once a week and exchange information. Talk about their research. It was pretty much her whole world when she wasn't working. She was really passionate about it and I guess he is too." She slapped her head and groaned. "Has anyone told him about Anita? I don't have his number but I can get it from Anita when she wakes up. He'll probably want to visit her in the hospital."

Jason exchanged a glance with his brother. Lita needed to be told the truth.

"Roger Gaines was shot three days ago," Jason said as gently and calmly as he could. "They found his body in the motor inn in Tremont. Do you know what he was doing there?"

Lita's face paled and her hands trembled as she scraped her fingers through her short hair. "He's dead? Are you sure?"

Very sure.

"I mean…are you sure it was Roger?" Lita said softly, more tears spilling over at the news.

"Yes, we're sure. That's why we wanted to speak to Anita. We wanted to know who might have wanted to hurt Roger. Did she ever talk to you about him?"

"Now and then. Like I said they worked on cases together. But they weren't romantic or anything," Lita added hastily. "It wasn't like that even if Roger said it was."

"Roger didn't tell us that Anita was his girlfriend. Roger's friend Brad Enright did. Did you ever meet him or hear about him?" West asked, leaning forward, his elbows on his knees.

"No. Never heard of him." Lita frowned. "You'll have to ask Anita when she wakes up. She had surgery last night. I stopped by this morning but she's still asleep."

Jason's phone vibrated. A text from Seth.

"Excuse me. I need to take this."

Jason stepped into the next room which turned out to be the kitchen to see what Seth had to say. His answer was quick and to the point.

Anita Hazlitt had been shot walking home from a study

session with friends last night. Serious injuries but doctors were optimistic. No witnesses. Why was Jason asking?

He'd call Seth and give him the whole story when they were done talking to Lita. Punching out a brief reply, Jason rejoined West and the young woman who looked even more frightened than she had when they first met her.

"Lita, do you know what case Anita and Roger were working on?"

This was the best lead they'd had so far. Perhaps Anita and Roger had been onto something. Or someone. Someone willing to kill to keep them silent.

"No, I didn't really listen that closely." Lita grabbed a tissue from the box on the end table and blew her nose. "But I think I know how I can find out. Anita was a little strange about the cases she worked on. She didn't leave anything around the house about them."

Which meant Seth's investigators wouldn't have found anything to help them identify the shooter.

"Where did she keep things?" West asked. "At work? Maybe her parents' house?"

Lita stood and walked over to a desk in the corner of the living room and rummaged through the middle drawer. "She'd never trust anyone that much. She kept everything hidden in her car."

As someone who had worked in the DEA for years, Jason knew very well there were several places a person could hide secrets in a vehicle. If Lita didn't know exactly where, Jason was sure he could find it.

Lita held up a single silver key. "This is to her trunk. She keeps everything under the spare tire."

Jason had to temper his excitement and stay calm despite wanting to grab the key and race down the stairs. This could be the "what" he and West had been waiting for.

A suspect and a damn motive.

"You lead the way and we'll follow." He and West stood, allowing Lita to walk ahead of them toward the door.

They needed to see whatever was hidden in Anita's car. Then they needed to talk to Seth and see if he had any suspects, plus let him know what they'd found out and how the two murders were probably linked. And last but not least, talk to Anita if and when she woke up and was able to speak and answer questions. That might not be for awhile.

But at least now they had a direction – a lead. Something they could work until they found the killer or another clue. They were in a better position than they'd been driving here.

Finally things were looking up.

✦ ✦ ✦

"SO HOW DO you know Jason?" Brinley asked as she and Logan Wright played blackjack out on Jason's back deck. It was another gorgeous sunny day and neither one of them had wanted to stay cooped up in the house. The repairmen had come and gone and now she had a shiny new door with a whale of a lock that would take a battering ram to knock it down.

Logan dealt her two cards, one face up and one face down before dealing himself the same.

"Work," Logan grunted, his eyes on his cards – a two and a

ten. "He's actually pretty close friends with Reed Mitchell but then we all started helping each other about five years ago. He was a damn good agent."

Brinley had no doubt about that. Jason would excel at everything he did. That's just who he was.

"Do you all do dangerous things?"

Logan chuckled at her question. "That's why I joined in partnership with Jason and Jared. I have a wife and kids and wanted to make sure I spent many happy years with them. But if you're asking if we've done dangerous things the answer is yes. But I don't think that's your real question. I think you want to know if we miss it."

She had a lousy poker face apparently. "Do you?"

"Sometimes. There's an adrenaline rush that you can't get anywhere else."

Brinley didn't think she'd felt an adrenaline rush like that in her entire life. Ever.

"Do you think Jason will go back to the DEA?"

"Doubtful. I think he's done with government bureaucracies. But maybe that's a question you should ask him," Logan replied. Her casual questioning clearly didn't fool him. He tapped her cards. "Are you holding?"

It appeared Logan was done answering personal queries about Jason. She shook her head. "Hit me."

Logan scowled and didn't deal the card. "You're supposed to stay on anything above sixteen or seventeen. You're going to go over."

"You don't know that for sure unless you're cheating," Brinley answered with a teasing smile. "So hit me."

A slow grin spread across Logan's face. "I like your style, Brinley Snow. Fearless. I'm not too fond of rules myself. You want a card, you got it."

Holding her breath, she waited as his hand seemed to move in slow motion. She was far from fearless. Stupid was probably a better word for it.

Three of spades. Logan laughed and shook his head.

"You have the luck with you today. Let's see if I do."

Logan dealt himself a king of clubs. Busted. She'd won. It was...unexpected.

"You looked shocked," Logan observed, gathering the cards up to reshuffle the deck. "If you thought you were going to lose why did you do it?"

That was an excellent question. One she wasn't sure she could explain but she'd try without going into all the gory details of her personal life.

"I was tired of playing it safe, following the rules," she said finally after a long pause. "It's what I've done my whole life and I just didn't want to do it anymore. And a card game with nothing riding on it seemed like a good time to try it out."

"You kind of remind me of my wife Ava," Logan said, rubbing his chin. "She got tired of that too. Her family had put her in a neat little box of who they thought she should be."

That sounded very familiar. "So what did she do?"

Logan flashed a wicked grin that probably melted the panties off of most women. "Took a ride on my motorcycle."

I just bet she did. The hotter than firecrackers lawman probably had to beat them off with a broom before he was married.

Brinley cleared her throat and tried to hold in her laughter.

"Is that some sort of euphemism?"

Logan gave her a blank look and then realization dawned along with amusement. "Nope, it was a real Harley. She said it felt like flying and she was right. There's nothing like the feeling of freedom. I highly recommend it if you're thinking about starting to color outside the lines."

Brinley liked the way he phrased it. Coloring outside the lines. It wasn't that she wanted to go on a crime spree and knock over a bank; she just wanted to take a few chances for a change. Stay up late. Eat ice cream for breakfast. Show up late to a movie and miss the previews.

Take a chance with a sexy wounded lawman named Jason Anderson.

"Hmmmm… A Harley riding second grade teacher. I would certainly make an impression on the parents."

"If you're going to take chances you have to stop worrying about what other people think about your decisions." Logan leaned forward, a smile playing on his lips. "I'm going to tell you a secret. Most people are so damn worried about themselves they don't have time to worry about what you're doing. And the few that do? They're not worth worrying about, always with their noses in other people's business. It'd be a better world if we stopped judging everybody by what they drive or how they're dressed. That's just my two cents, of course."

"I haven't taken many chances in my life," Brinley sighed, knowing Logan was right. "I'm a big fraidy-cat."

"Funny, but you don't act like one. You've taken this entire murder thing in stride. Most people would have started drinking or curled up into a ball and watched twenty hours of television straight. You, on the other hand, stood up and told my stubborn partner that you wanted to help find the killer. That, my new friend, takes guts. No fraidy-cat would do that."

"You're a nice man, Logan Wright."

"Don't let that get around. I have a reputation to protect." He began to shuffle the cards. "Are we still playing?"

Brinley grinned and slapped the table. "Absolutely. I'm going to play like there are no rules."

Words to live by.

Chapter Fifteen

"WE'VE HAD THIS all wrong," Jason groaned as he, West, and Seth paged through Anita's notes. They were sitting in the interrogation room at Seth's station and what they were learning turned everything upside down.

"It's the house. Roger and Anita were investigating Brinley's house," West said, rubbing his temple. "Or at least what happened in that house. How did I not know about this? I'm the damn lead detective in Tremont."

"I don't go through our cold cases very often," Seth shrugged. "I don't have the manpower, to be honest. Unless something comes up with one of them the chances of getting any resources is slim. It's sad but it's the truth. Presley scanned all our files in so if we do have a murder or missing person we can run a query in the database and look for crimes with a similar MO."

"That would be heaven." West tossed back the last of his soda. "Can I borrow Presley for a few months? I'd pay her well. If that crazy mayor will let me."

Seth grinned but shook his head. "She'd love the challenge but she's been pretty wore out these days being pregnant, having a toddler plus helping out here a couple of days a week. But she's always happy to train someone on how to do it. A few months ago she worked with Griffin's admin assistant."

"I may take you up on that," West promised, holding up a piece of paper. "But in the meantime I need to pull everything we can about the Barnes murder twenty years ago. This is the best motive we've found so far."

Jason slumped in his chair, his mind whirling with what they'd discovered. "This is not going to go over very well with Brinley. She bought that place as her dream house. I doubt the real estate agent revealed that there had been an unsolved murder there."

"You didn't know when you moved in next door?" Seth asked with a frown. "I thought you'd lived in Tremont your entire life."

"I would have been in college." Jason stroked his chin. "You too, West. If anyone mentioned a murder there I sure as hell don't remember it. Gail never talked about it. I admit she and I only had a few conversations when she lived there but she never mentioned that her sister was killed."

West pushed a piece of paper toward Jason. "Maybe no one mentioned it because they thought they had it solved. According to Anita's notes the cops always thought Linda Barnes was shot by her husband Wendell, but they could never prove it."

"Was he arrested?" Seth paged through the notes.

"No, and they never found the weapon. I saw that…here." Jason pulled out a copy of what appeared to be the original police report. "They picked him up the night of the murder by Tremont Lake. He said he was fishing. At night. They think he was getting rid of the gun. They didn't have much on this guy except a theory that Linda was spending him into the poor house so he shot her. If that was his only option he doesn't have great problem solving skills."

"Murderers rarely do. In a domestic situation we always look at the spouse first," Seth pointed out. "It looks like Roger and Anita were on to something that might prove his guilt. More motive and opportunity evidence. I guess we know who to talk to next."

"There's good news out of all of this." West nodded to Jason. "This doesn't have anything to do with Brinley personally. She doesn't need to fear for her life."

That fact was already making breathing a hell of a lot easier for Jason. She didn't need to be babysat every moment of the day but he was still planning to keep a close eye on her.

But now for purely personal reasons.

One thing still bugged him though.

"Someone did try to break into her house when she wasn't there. Was it the killer? Or was it completely random? I know what my vote is so I think I'll keep her at my house until we solve this."

West's lips twitched. "Better safe than sorry. I'm sure you'll take real good care of Ms. Snow."

Seth scratched his head. "Did I miss something here?"

West looked down at the notes in his hand but Jason could still see the shit-eating grin on his brother's face.

"Jason has a girlfriend," West whispered, his shoulders shaking with laughter.

"Aww, hell," Jason growled. "It's like we're back in junior

high or something."

If only that was the case. Things had been a whole lot simpler back then. His biggest concern was getting to second base. As a grown man he had more complex desires.

And he could only hope Brinley was his girlfriend. She was the most interesting woman Jason had met in years. Maybe ever.

Now that she was out of the line of fire it was time to turn up the volume on the wooing. Dazzle her with some real romance. She deserved better than he'd given her so far.

Jason was ready to take a chance on Brinley Snow.

✦ ✦ ✦

JASON WAS FLIPPING burgers at the grill flanked by West and Logan while Brinley relaxed and sipped a glass of wine. A drink she'd desperately needed after hearing about Jason's day and what he had found. The best news being that she wasn't a target. Roger Gaines had her address in his hand because of the house. Not because of her.

Of course now her dream home was the scene of some horrific unsolved murder.

That sucked.

It made Brinley want to call that real estate agent up and give her a piece of her mind. Except that if Brinley hadn't moved into the house then she probably wouldn't have met Jason. She couldn't have one without the other.

Brinley took another fortifying sip of her wine. "So she was shot in the hallway? By her husband? I wonder if the house is haunted."

Jason paused from adding cheese to the hamburgers. "Have you seen any ghosts or had anything strange happen?"

"No."

Jason grinned and took a big bite out of a slice of cheddar. "Then it's not haunted. And we don't know that it was her husband. He said it must have been an intruder because some jewels and money were missing."

"That makes sense."

For some reason Brinley didn't want to think the poor woman had been shot by a man she loved.

"Except that the jewels never showed up in any pawn shops or guys fencing stolen goods. If they stole the jewelry they didn't do anything with it," West pointed out. "Why steal something if you're never going to use it?"

"People steal art paintings just so they can possess them." Logan plucked a potato chip from the bowl on the table. "It's what it represents more than the money."

"So you think the husband did it then?" Huck plopped his head on her knee and she gave him a scratch behind his ears.

"The police seemed to think so but they didn't have much evidence to go with their theory. At this point I could go either way." West paged through the file folder he'd brought from police headquarters. "It's really kind of sad that there's so little here. It doesn't reflect well on the detectives working twenty years ago."

"No witnesses. No murder weapon. Conflicting statements and a victim others really didn't like much. A cop's worst nightmare," Logan mused. "Add in the fact that small town cops didn't have much in the way of DNA back then. You might want to cut them some slack."

West's lips twisted and he shut the folder with a snap. "You're right. They talked to the neighbors, friends, everyone they could think of. They went over the house with a fine-tooth comb. No fingerprints or hairs that shouldn't be there, which is one of the reasons they were leaning toward the husband. The whole thing is sad. It tore the family apart from what I can see."

"Family?" Brinley frowned as Jason piled burgers on a platter and set them in the middle of the table. "Did they have children? What happened to them?"

"One child. A son from Wendell Barnes's first marriage." Jason waved a spatula toward the file. "Damian Barnes was a teenager when it happened. Out with friends at a movie. He's the one that found the body."

Brinley shuddered. "Ugh. I imagine that would stay with you the rest of your life. Did you know him?"

West frowned and shook his head. "Jason and I were older. In college when he was in high school." West scribbled something on a piece of paper. "We'll need to talk to him and the father. And of course Gail Denton. I know she's over at the assisted living place but I have no idea where the other two ended up."

Logan piled his burger high with pickles, lettuce and tomato. "Follow the money. From what I read the family is loaded. Would your parents know the Barnes or remember them?"

Jason sat down and joined the rest of them around the table. "That's a good question. Maybe I should show up at Sunday dinner tomorrow and find out."

West groaned and slumped in his chair. "Don't even say

that. If you go and start asking questions they're going to ask where I am. Shit."

"Why don't you want to go?" Brinley asked, although she couldn't keep from smiling at West's comically tortured expression. From the little she'd heard from Jason the Anderson family was close-knit and quite happy.

"They ask him when he's going to settle down and give them grandchildren," Jason laughed and winked at Brinley. "Mom is always trying to fix him up."

"The only reason she's given up on you is–" West's grin immediately died and everyone fell silent, the levity from only moments ago completely gone, leaving a grim tension in its wake.

Jason looked around the table, his expression somber. "We all know why so there's no reason to pretend. Let's get back to the case. That's what is really important." He turned to West. "Can you find the Barnes family or should I put Jared on it?"

"We can find them. Logan's right. We'll follow the money. But it wouldn't hurt to ask Mom and Dad what they remember about the case."

Jason shook his fork at West playfully. "We'll both ask them. Together."

West took a long draw from his beer. "I hope it's pot roast. That would make it worth it."

"Then maybe tomorrow while you two are with your family I'll go over and give my house a good top to bottom cleaning. I haven't had a chance since the break in."

Three sets of eyes swung toward Brinley and she squirmed under their incredulous gaze. Finally Jason spoke.

"Absolutely not. Someone broke in. Why we don't know, but it still isn't safe for you to be alone over there. You'll come with us tomorrow."

Go with them to meet Mommy and Daddy?

Absolutely not. No way. Not going to happen.

Chapter Sixteen

BRINLEY LOOKED READY to bolt back to the car. Her usual sunny smile was replaced with a frown of worry despite Jason's assurances that his parents were friendly people. Hell, if they thought he was serious with Brinley they'd probably fall all over themselves to welcome her into the family. Jason's mother was desperate to see him happy and settled after everything he'd been through.

Brinley looked lovely today in a flowered sundress that showed off her golden skin and luscious curves. She'd left her long brown hair loose and it hung in waves to the middle of her back, making his fingers itch to run his hands through it. He had a distinct memory from the other night regarding how silky it felt.

Jason hugged his mother and shook hands with his father but both his parents were paying attention to the woman behind him. He stepped aside and wrapped an arm around Brinley's waist, pulling her forward.

"Mom. Dad. I'd like you to meet a good friend, Brinley Snow. She moved into the house next to mine. Brinley, this is my mother and father, Marie and Peter Anderson."

"It's nice to meet you both." Brinley shook hands with his parents while Jason's mother kept giving him excited sidelong glances. Marie Anderson thought this was the big introduction. That Brinley was *the one.* Jason would have to pull his mother aside today and let her know as gently as he could that Brinley had only come into his life a short time ago. It was much too soon to be declaring anything serious. Although if he were going to get serious, Brinley would be exactly the kind of woman he'd want.

"Brinley. What an unusual name," Marie exclaimed as she took Brinley by the hand and led her into the dining room. "You're the first I've met. Is it a family name, dear?"

Brinley looked nervously over her shoulder at Jason as she was being led away like a lamb to slaughter. Before Marie Anderson was done she'd know every little detail about Brinley, including her grandmother's maiden name. His mother had missed her calling. She should have worked for the NSA.

Jason felt a little guilty but he knew better than to interfere with his mother when she had a goal in mind. If he and Brinley had any sort of future, and he didn't even know if that's what he wanted, she'd need to learn how to handle his mother.

"No, just one my parents liked. Something smells wonderful. Is it pot roast?"

"It is. Do you like to cook?" Marie didn't wait for an answer, continuing to lead Brinley away from Jason. "Why don't you come into the kitchen and we can talk recipes?"

Jason, West, and his father watched the two women disappear behind the swinging door to the kitchen in silence.

"Do you think we'll ever see Brinley again?" West said in a

mock serious tone. "Poor girl. She has no idea that she's being pumped for information and vetted as the future Mrs. Jason Anderson. If she did, she'd run out the door and never look back."

Peter Anderson slapped Jason on the back and smiled. "I'm sure your girl will be fine. How long have you two been together?"

"She'd not exactly my girl. We're…friends. Good friends."

A friend that Jason had kissed. And fantasized about seeing naked.

His father gave him a knowing look. "Of course. Friends. Well, she seems like a nice girl. Very pretty. You said she's your neighbor?"

"She lives in Gail Denton's old place. Which leads me to a question, Dad. What do you know about the Barnes family and the murder that took place there twenty years ago?"

"Does Dad need a lawyer?"

Jason hadn't heard his oldest brother enter the house but that query had come from Travis Anderson who ran the business side of the family holdings. Tall and dark-haired just like the rest of the Anderson clan, he leaned heavily on a cane due to hip surgery after a motorcycle accident a year ago. Pain was etched on Travis's face, making him look older than his forty-two years but he was still smiling, albeit with difficulty.

"No attorney required. I was just wondering what he remembered," Jason replied as he hugged his brother. "It's good to see you. I thought you were still in New York."

Travis was spending time in the Big Apple working with a rehab specialist.

"I've been home for several days. You and West have been busy with your new case."

"You heard about it then?" West asked as they sat down in the living room. "Do you remember anything about the Barnes family?"

Travis rubbed his chin and set his cane down on the floor, sliding it behind his feet. "I remember Wendell Barnes coming here to the house a few times but that's it. I don't think I ever met his wife."

Peter Anderson stood and strode over to the bar in the corner of the room. Silver-haired but still vital and energetic in his mid-sixties, he'd been the driving force behind Anderson Industries since its inception forty years ago. What had started as progressive ranching had grown into mining, oil, and banking making their father one of the richest men in Montana, if not the entire western half of the country.

"If we're going to talk about that murder twenty years ago I'm going to have to have a drink. Anyone want to join me?"

Peter poured four glasses of whiskey and West helped him pass out the drinks before they all sat back down.

"So you do remember the murder." Jason tossed back the liquor, enjoying the burn all the way down to his belly. "I guess we were all at college."

"All three of you boys were gone at the time. It was a terrible thing, really. Everyone in town knew that Linda and Dell had marital problems. Linda loved to spend money and she was frustrated with Dell's ideas about living a frugal life. She hated that house. Thought it was way too small. She wanted something she could throw lavish parties in and decorate expensively. Never made a secret about it either. Her complaints were loud and frequent to anyone who would listen."

"So everyone thought Wendell did it?" West prompted. "Did you?"

"No, but I don't know if I would call Dell a nice man either. He could be ruthless in business and he definitely didn't lack self-esteem. But a murderer? I doubt it. From what I remember he hated guns. He only had them in the house for protection. They'd been robbed a few times."

Robbed more than once in a town like Tremont? That alone was strange.

West cleared his throat noisily. "So you say Wendell didn't like guns, Dad? And that they'd been robbed? That wasn't in the police report."

"Dell hated guns. He begrudgingly bought one when they were robbed about six months before Linda was shot." Tom frowned and took another sip of his whiskey. "I don't remember what the burglars took though."

"The cops found him at the lake. He said he was fishing in the middle of the night. Was he a fisherman?"

Tom sighed and shook his head. "Not that I ever heard of. But that doesn't mean he didn't. We weren't close friends, only acquaintances. Maybe Damian was into fishing."

"What happened to him?" Jason's fingers tightened around the highball glass. So far he hadn't learned anything earthshattering. "The file doesn't say a thing and I don't remember him at all."

"He was younger, of course." Peter rubbed his chin in thought. "A nice boy. Very smart. When Linda died Dell sent him off to boarding school in upstate New York. I don't think he ever came to visit his Aunt Gail, which is a shame. She's a sweet woman and deserved better treatment than she got by Wendell."

It looked like there was plenty of animosity to go around in the Barnes family. But if Jason could finally solve Linda Barnes's murder, he would bet that he would solve Roger Gaines's at the same time.

"I'll be talking to Gail," Jason revealed. "And I'm going to need to talk to Wendell and Damian as well. Plus anyone else who might have had a motive."

"It's a two for one. We find one killer it will lead us to the other." West finished his whiskey and slapped it down on the coffee table. His father went back to the bar and poured himself another.

Travis picked up his cane and struggled to his feet.

"Neither Wendell nor Linda were very well liked in this community. Some people might not want to walk down that memory lane with you so be careful."

"Like who?" West asked, getting to his feet. "I'm not giving the rich and powerful a pass on this investigation."

"I have a distinct memory of Wendell in the study with Dad and another man. Wendell and that man were at each other's throats and Dad was trying to keep the peace."

"So who was it?" Jason stood as well, too restless to sit still.

Travis grinned, the look of pain and fatigue temporarily falling away. "Mayor Leon Cavendish. Of course he wasn't the mayor then. Have fun questioning him."

West groaned and slapped his forehead. "Shit. Just…shit."

Jason and West were about to dig up a few buried secrets in this town, and it was not going to go over well.

✦ ✦ ✦

"SO HOW LONG have you known Jason?"

Marie Anderson was probably somewhere in her sixties but looked ten years younger. Her eyes were the same shade of green as Jason's and she had the same easy smile. The older woman had been delicately asking Brinley questions about her family, Chicago, and teaching but apparently the pussyfooting was over and done. The questions were becoming more direct and she didn't mind a bit. Of course Jason's mother would want to know who her son was spending time with.

"Not long actually. Until the whole…well, murder thing…we were really just acquaintances. Waving and smiling as we went about our lives."

"Such a sad incident. And you say you didn't know this man at all?" Marie Anderson pulled the roast from the oven and then sat down at the table with Brinley. "We'll let that rest for a few minutes and then serve dinner."

"Not at all. He was a complete stranger. But that's why I want to get to the bottom of this."

"I thought you had." Marie frowned in confusion. "You said he had your address because of the murder that took place there twenty years ago."

Brinley blushed and shifted in her chair. "Well, yes, but I want to know who killed him and why. Was he shot because of what he knew about Linda Barnes or is it another reason?

Something completely unrelated?"

"You sound like my sons," Marie laughed. "Since they were kids they've been curious. It wasn't a surprise when West and Jason went into law enforcement."

"They seem like they know their jobs."

A strange expression passed over Marie Anderson's face, leaving behind a shadow of sadness.

"I'm not unhappy that Jason left the DEA. I always worried about him. And then of course the worst really did happen. We had no idea what happened to him for weeks. I thought…"

Brinley couldn't stop herself from reaching out to this woman. "I can't imagine what you've been through. The waiting. Not knowing. It must have been a nightmare."

Her eyes bright with unshed tears, Marie nodded. "A parent wants their child to be happy and healthy. But I knew that if they hadn't already killed him that he was neither of those things. You should have seen him when he first escaped. Thin as a rail and covered in sores and cuts. He spent some time in the hospital also because he was severely dehydrated."

Brinley squeezed Marie's hand. "He's a strong man."

Jason's mother took a deep breath and smiled. "All my boys are, my daughter Leann too. They get that from their father. Still, I worry about Jason. I can't imagine that a person could go through something like that and not be changed in some way."

Brinley didn't want to mention how Jason couldn't sleep so many nights.

"Time is a great healer," she said instead, feeling awkward knowing something Marie Anderson didn't know.

"Yes, it is. Will you be there?" the older woman asked with a shrewd look on her face. “I know I’m being nosey and it’s none of my business, but will you be around in the future? I think you might be just what Jason needs.”

Brinley didn’t know how to respond. She didn’t have the answer herself. They were playing it day by day, not looking too far ahead. The good Lord knew Brinley had feelings for Jason. Strong ones.

“I’ll be there as long as he needs me,” Brinley found herself answering. It was at least honest. Even if they weren’t romantically involved she would always want to be his friend. He’d only been in her life a few days really, but already she couldn’t imagine a life without him. “He’s done so much to help me. I want to help him too.”

Jason’s mother smiled in satisfaction so she must have liked the answer well enough. “Good then. If you want to go through I’ll bring out the meal. I know the men are probably chomping at the bit for dinner.”

Brinley felt like she’d passed some sort of test that she hadn’t been given an opportunity to study for. Or at least the first hurdle.

If she wanted a future with Jason his mother wouldn’t stand in their way.

Which was good news.

The only question now was…did Brinley want a future with Jason? Signs were pointing to yes.

Chapter Seventeen

"YOUR PARENTS ARE nice," Brinley said as they drove away from the Anderson family home. She hadn't been happy at first about attending their traditional Sunday dinner but his family was friendly and charming. "You and your brothers look so much alike too."

"I guess we do look like Dad. I think my sister Leann looks like Mom. She's working in Florida right now so that's why she wasn't there today."

"It sounds like you were close growing up."

Brinley had been close to her brother and sister when they were young but as they grew older their lives seemed to diverge.

"I am with my brothers but Leann came along much later so we're not as close as we could be. Honestly, we didn't have much choice," Jason laughed. "Three boys in five years stretched my parents to the limit – emotionally, physically, and financially. Dad was just starting out then and they didn't have much money. Mom helped do the ranch books and took care of us. That wasn't an easy task. We were typical boys and I swear one of us was in trouble at least once a day. The house we had then was small and the three of us shared a room. Mom never sent anyone to their room as a punishment because then the other two would go in there and the next thing she knew we'd be rolling around and wrestling or something. She had to get creative. Punishments were much more participatory. Cleaning out the garage or scrubbing garbage cans."

Not once had Brinley wrestled with a sibling. She couldn't imagine her sister even getting her clothes dirty. And her brother the muscle factory would have had her pinned in seconds.

Cleaning trash cans sounded smelly and gross.

"My mother would give us a timeout but I didn't get punished very often. There wasn't much trouble to get ino and I didn't have a smart mouth or anything."

In fact, Brinley had always tried to make her parents happy, not give them a hard time.

Jason glanced at her before returning his gaze to the road. "That's the saddest thing I've ever heard, honey. You need to raise some hell. And I think I know just that place."

Grinning from ear to ear, he quickly changed lanes and did a U-turn on the two lane road. Her pulse quickened at the idea of doing something exciting. Something…naughty.

"Did Logan say something to you?"

"No, should he have?"

The sun was setting behind the trees and normally she'd be in for the evening, either reading or maybe watching television. But not tonight. She was going to do something out of the ordinary and with this very extraordinary man.

"I–I just mentioned that I didn't want to play it safe so much. I wanted to take a few chances," she admitted. "Not anything dangerous. Just not be so predictable all the time."

"I don't think you're predictable in the least," Jason declared. "And this won't be dangerous, I promise. We're going to have some fun. I think we both need it after the last several days thinking you were in danger. Now that we know that you're not we can relax and enjoy ourselves. Do you trust me?"

She'd trusted him with her life, so trusting him with some fun was a no-brainer. She couldn't wait to raise some hell with the best looking man in Tremont.

Bring it on.

✦ ✦ ✦

THE BEAT FROM the band inside could be felt all the way to the sidewalk. Brinley's hand was firmly entwined with Jason's but her heart was still racing with trepidation. The sign outside the building said this was "Harley's Honkytonk. Good eats, cold beer, and pretty girls."

"You'll love this place," Jason assured her as he pulled the door open and a blast of music almost knocked her on her ass. He had to lean down right next to her ear so she could hear him. "Some friends of mine play here every Friday, Saturday, and Sunday night."

"We're going to dance?"

She let Jason lead her through a labyrinth of tables and people, all of whom seemed to know him. Several times someone yelled out his name or slapped him on the back. She could feel the eyes of the patrons looking her over, probably to decide if she measured up to the other women he'd brought here. Or even if she was attractive enough to be one of the "pretty girls" the neon sign outside had boasted of.

The song ended and the thirsty dancing couples seemed to move as a unit toward the bar, leaving a pathway to a large table near the stage. Jason pulled out a chair for her as three of the men from the band greeted Jason as if he were their long-lost brother. After they'd ribbed him about how long it had been since they'd seen him, he placed his hands on Brinley's shoulders.

"Guys, I'd like you to meet Brinley Snow. Brinley, this is Floyd Martin, he plays bass. That's Henry Gatille, he plays drums. The tall one there is Chance Morton, he plays keyboards, and the ugly one bringing the beers is Zeke Dougal. He's on guitar."

"I ain't near as ugly as you," Zeke laughed and hugged Jason after handing out the longnecks. "Where in the hell you been lately? Sunday nights aren't the same without you."

Brinley shook hands with the men who all seemed nice and normal. She'd never known anyone who played in a band but these men seemed just like regular guys. Jason had good taste in friends.

"Getting the business started has been a lot of work." Jason sat in the chair next to Brinley's and signaled for the waitress. "You know how it is."

The pretty blonde server leaned in, her bosom on full display in her low-cut white blouse she'd paired with a skin tight black skirt that showed a great deal of thigh.

"Hey, Jason. We've missed you in here." The waitress's voice was husky and seductive, and Brinley couldn't help but stiffen with indignation as the woman licked her lips in invitation.

To Jason.

The man that Brinley was with. Was she invisible or something? Or so ugly no one would believe that she was with a man as sexy as Jason Anderson? Maybe they thought she was some pity date or that he'd lost a bet.

"Nice to see you, Nell." Jason's arm settled around her shoulders, pulling her chair closer so she was sitting between his splayed legs while his other hand rested on her bare knee, his breath warm on her neck. "Honey, what do you want to drink?"

"Um, I guess a beer." She had a feeling this bar didn't serve too many of the martinis she'd been fond of in Chicago. In fact, she was quite out of place. She'd never been to a place called a honkytonk and it was clear that the waitress wished Brinley wasn't there at all.

Jason smiled and leaned down so his words were only for her. "Can you do Jake a favor and order something exotic? He's always complaining that he never gets to make a real cocktail around here. He moved here from New York and had some nightclub there. What did you order in Chicago?"

"A Cosmopolitan," she admitted, keeping her voice low. "But I'm okay with a beer, Jason."

"Jake will love it." Jason chuckled and dropped a kiss on her shoulder, leaving heat in its wake. "Nell, we'll have a longneck and a Cosmopolitan. Also bring a large cheese pizza and a bucket of hot wings."

"We just ate." Brinley eyed Jason's trim and muscular form in shock. He had to have the metabolism of a bumblebee.

"That was over two hours ago. Besides, you can't come to Harley's without trying the pizza and wings. They're legendary in these parts."

Zeke raised his bottle with a grin. "The sauce is so hot it'll put hair on your chest."

That was the last place she wanted to grow hair. Like most females, she spent more than her share of time ridding herself of hair in the regular places.

"So how do you all know each other?" Brinley asked as Nell sashayed toward the bar, several male admirers in her wake. What Brinley wouldn't give to be that sexually confident. The woman knew she was beautiful and played it for all it was worth.

"We grew up together," the man named Chance said. At least she thought it was Chance. The introductions had happened so fast it was all a blur. "And of course we all played on Tremont High's football team."

"You were a football player?" Brinley elbowed Jason, who looked more relaxed than she had ever seen him. "What position?"

"He was the pretty boy quarterback," Zeke snickered before Jason could answer. "We were his offensive line. He's the reason I can tell when it's going to rain because my knee hurts."

"If it hadn't been for me it would have been for someone else. You could have played quarterback if you wanted to. Everybody got the same chance to try out."

It didn't appear that the ribbing bothered Jason in the least. Brinley guessed it wasn't the first time he'd heard it.

"So did the team do well?" Brinley asked, remembering when her own brother's high school football team had won the state championships his junior and senior year. It was a big moment in a young man's life.

Everyone's face fell except for Chance's. He threw back his head, laughing at her seemingly innocent question. "We sucked. Really badly. I think our best record was four and four. But that didn't stop us from having a good time."

The drinks were slid in front of them, Nell lingering a little longer when she placed the bottle in front of Jason.

"Let me know if you need anything else," she purred in Jason's ear before drifting to the next table.

Brinley was getting tired of being ignored. Or disrespected. Either way it wasn't a classy way for a woman to act around another female. In a million years she would never act like that around a guy with a girl sitting right next to him.

Looking over her shoulder at the waitress, Brinley tightened her grip on Jason's hand to get his attention.

"Is there some history with you and her that I'm not aware of?"

He gave her an abashed look. "She and I dated for a little while in high school. That's it, I swear. But she's like that with everybody, not just me."

Brinley arched her brow at this man who was looking pretty embarrassed. "Really? She didn't act like that with me. She didn't do it with the other guys or the people at that table. I don't like it when women don't respect other women. I saw that all the time at my sister's pageants."

"Nell knows nothing is going to ever happen between us." Jason caressed the skin of her bare arm, sending tingles straight to her toes. "She does that to feel better about herself. She's had a hard time of things. A divorce. But you're right—it's not respectful. I guess people around here have just gotten used to it.

If you want me to say something to her I will."

"No." Brinley shook her head, feeling crappy now that she'd heard more about Nell's life. "I'm overreacting because of the things I've seen. You weren't disrespectful to me at any point and honestly that's all I care about."

"I'll never do that." His expression was solemn and truthful. He leaned closer, his words only for her. "This means something to me, honey."

Her throat tightened and she laid her head on his shoulder, snuggling as close as she could to his warm body. He smelled delicious, a mixture of citrus and spice that made her head spin and her heart pound.

"It means something to me too."

The other guys got to their feet and lumbered back onto the stage, their first song a cover of one of her favorite Rascal Flatts tunes. For the first time in days Brinley truly relaxed, letting the music carry all her troubles away. At that moment she wasn't a woman with a murder problem and he wasn't the ex-cop trying to help her. They were just two people – a man and a woman – having a wonderful time.

The song came to an end and Zeke stepped up to the microphone. "Thank you, everybody. I hope you all can help me tonight. We have a good friend in the audience who sometimes joins in but he might need some convincing. How about we put our hands together and convince Jason Anderson to come up on stage?"

The applause was thunderous. Bar patrons stood, some even on the tables and chairs, clapping, whistling, and calling his name to exhort Jason to hop up on stage. Whether he played an instrument or sang she had no idea, but clearly her date was embarrassed. He'd groaned and then ducked down so he was hiding behind her shoulder.

"Damn that Zeke. He's always pulling shit like this."

"Is he serious? Do you really join in?"

The entire crowd looked like it might riot if he didn't do it, and she couldn't deny she was bursting with curiosity herself. She wanted to see him up on stage performing.

"Sometimes. We had a band in high school."

Jason was still hunched over, his elbows on his knees. Brinley looked over her shoulder at the rabid fans screaming for a show.

"If you don't get up there I doubt we'll get out of here alive. And I have a lot to live for."

She'd made a joke but actually she was semi-serious. This crowd wasn't going to take no for an answer.

"Aww, hell. I'm sorry, honey." Jason stood and bounded up on stage. Holding his hands up, the crowd quieted down enough for him to speak. "Thanks, everyone. Maybe just one tonight."

Brinley didn't know what to expect so when he and the band launched into Todd Rungren's "Hello, It's Me" her mouth fell open in shock. Jason's voice was good. Better than good, it was excellent. He'd been handed another guitar and was playing alongside Zeke and clearly having a ball.

Her boyfriend was a freakin' rock star.

He looked every inch the part up on stage, a sheen of sweat on his face and neck. Handsome and sinfully sexy in a pair of well-worn jeans and a button down shirt, he belted out the lyrics as if he'd done it a thousand times. For all she knew…he had.

And she was every inch the starry-eyed groupie watching him

strut his stuff. She couldn't tear her gaze away as the band moved into their version of Tim McGraw's "Real Good Man". She had to wipe the drool from her chin as Jason gripped the microphone, his cowboy hat casting a shadow over his face under the hot stage lights.

She was caught in his web so securely that when he hopped off the stage and came right up to her, pulling her to her feet and laying a kiss on her lips, she didn't once protest or even demure. With the raucous crowd screaming and stomping their boots, she allowed the sexiest man she'd ever met to sweep her off her feet.

And then some.

Because when she finally came back to earth, she wasn't watching from the audience. She was standing at the steps to the stage, right next to him, and he was urging her up the stairs.

"You wanted to take a chance, honey." Jared was grinning ear to ear. "I've heard you sing when you do yard work. You have a great voice."

"Jason Anderson, you are out of your mind," she hissed while still trying to smile. Strangely enough with the lights directed at the stage, she couldn't see past the first row of people. Everyone else was a black mass of sound. "I can't sing up there."

"Why not? I promise you'll feel like you can climb a mountain when you're done. It isn't dangerous but you are definitely doing something out of the ordinary. Something remarkable."

She wanted to be pissed off at him but she wasn't. After all, she'd said she wanted to get out of her comfort zone. Take chances. Live life to the fullest. But she'd been thinking smaller. Much smaller. Maybe waiting until the day her power bill was due to pay it. Things like that.

"What will everyone think?" Even as the words came out of her mouth she realized how silly she sounded. She'd lived too long in the slot her parents had created for her. She'd worried about what they would think. What her friends would think.

Anyone that would judge her harshly wasn't someone who cared. This was a chance to be brave and he was holding it out to her on a silver platter. The only question was whether she had the guts to grab it with both hands.

"Everyone is probably too drunk to think anything past how fucking gorgeous you look. But I won't drag you up there with me if you don't want to go."

The crowd was hooting and hollering. The band was smiling and beckoning, and even Jason looked encouraging. She wanted to do it. But she also wanted to crawl back to her chair and stay out of the limelight.

Like her whole life. She'd lived in the shadows of both her brother and sister. It could get cold and dark there. Jason was offering a chance at something else. This was the entire reason she'd moved to Montana.

Brinley placed her hand in his and smiled before she lost her nerve.

"Let's do this."

Chapter Eighteen

BRINLEY SOARED ON a rush of endorphins. Terrified but resolute, she'd taken her place on stage next to Jason. Chance had asked what song she wanted to sing and she'd opened her mouth but nothing came out even as her heart galloped in her chest and a fresh spate of sweat broke out on the back of her neck. Jason had suggested "Remind Me", a song originally sung by Carrie Underwood and Brad Paisley that she luckily knew the words to. As the band swung into the song Brinley had been standing on two trembling legs, but something in the way Jason looked at her helped her through the first few notes.

Then it was off to the races.

The exultant feeling that suffused every pore of her being as she sang with Jason simply could not be described. Nor could she believe the crash of applause when they finished that hit her like a freight train and shook her out of the dream-like state she'd been drifting in. Jason lifted her up and swung her around jubilantly and she clung to his wide shoulders, already drunk from her scary walk on the wild side.

"You are something else, Brinley Snow."

Jason's deep and husky voice reached her ears despite the decibel level in the bar. He led her down the stage stairs and toward the exit with congratulations and well wishes on the way. By the time they hit the door the cooler night air glided over her skin like silk. She lifted her long hair off her neck and smiled up at the man who had taken her farther than anyone else. He'd brought out a side of her she didn't even know existed.

"Are you mad at me? I never would have dragged you up there. Not in a million years. But I wanted you to feel what it's like to really walk on the edge."

Jason looked so worried she reached up and stroked the deep grooves in his forehead. She was far from angry. He was right. She felt powerful. And strong. Facing fear did that to a person. So did coming into the light.

"I'm not mad. Not even close. You were right, you know. I want to climb a mountain. I want to run a marathon. I want to paint a masterpiece. I want to roll around in a field of flowers."

They were both laughing at her flight of fancy but it didn't change how empowered she felt at the moment. She didn't have to live in anyone's shadow any longer.

"I've got some begonias in the backyard." Jason stroked his chin playfully. "You're welcome to roll around in those. Then we can take a few laps around the block if you like. And the back deck has been needing another coat of paint, although it might not be a masterpiece when we're done."

Her heart pounded as she gazed at this man that had become special so quickly. Always before she'd played it safe. Waiting until she knew the man's feelings before she tipped her own hand. Dragging her feet to intimacy, telling herself that men weren't worth the hassle and heartache.

But this one was. It might not be love but damn it…it meant something. More. Than anything had before. She wouldn't hesitate this time. Grabbing his hand, she led him toward the truck. She had plans, and she wasn't thinking small now.

"Take me home," she said simply and his dazzling smile seemed to say he was thinking exactly the same thing.

Brinley couldn't wait to be with Jason and to take another chance.

✦ ✦ ✦

BRINLEY HAD TO easily be the most beautiful woman Jason had ever laid eyes on. He'd watched in fascination as her entire face lit up and her eyes glowed when they'd sang together. It was an incredibly intimate thing to do in front of a crowd of people, but after the first few bars he hadn't even been aware of the prying eyes. They'd been two people alone.

Except they weren't, really.

He'd laid a couple of pretty big kiss on her pink, full lips in front of the rowdiest crowd in Tremont – which wasn't like him – and she hadn't batted an eyelash. She'd simply given as good as she got, making him ache to make love to her. Strip their clothes and do unspeakably carnal things to one another.

He'd been delighted as she'd dragged him to the truck, her hand on his thigh all the way home. It hadn't been easy to concentrate with a raging hard-on but luckily Sunday night traffic was light and they'd pulled into his driveway safe, sound, and eager.

He only had one destination in mind when he unlocked the front door but Huck had other plans. The excited, wriggling canine was happy to see them, licking and barking with joy at their arrival. The overgrown puppy also needed to go outside.

He'd had his paws crossed apparently, although Jason hadn't let him alone longer than he knew Huck could handle. All in all it had been about five hours but the dog was acting like it had been five years as he watered those begonias between running back to his master for cuddles.

"I'm sorry about this," Jason apologized. "You know how Huck is when we first get home."

"I know. I can wait." Her voice was soft and full of promise. Jason's cock pressed insistently against his button fly even as his heart accelerated to a full gallop. "I'll be inside."

Jason couldn't rush Huck through the normal paces no matter how much he wanted to. The dog did his business and Jason made sure there were plenty of belly rubs and ear scratches before they both came in. With Brinley nowhere in the living room or kitchen, Jason tossed Huck a doggy treat, turned on the television, and rushed to the master bedroom. His furry roommate would crash on the nearest soft couch or chair, snoring softly while reruns of *Big Bang Theory* played in the background.

One sight of Brinley lying on his bed wearing nothing but a black lace and satin panty and bra set had Jason almost swallowing his tongue. Her long brown hair was swept over one shoulder and she was looking at him with invitation in her eyes. It had been a long time since he'd been with anyone that he cared about. He didn't know exactly what his feelings for Brinley were but he did know she was special. Tonight wasn't just any other night.

"Is Huck okay?"

Jason's fogged brain took a moment to remember who the hell Huck was. His blood supply had pooled in his groin making it very hard to think clearly.

"He's fine. He likes to lie on the sofa and sleep."

"He's not allowed on the sofa."

"That's why he likes to do it." Jason took a few steps closer to the bed, his gaze never wavering from Brinley's luscious form. "God, you are gorgeous. I don't even know where to start."

Looking up at him from under her lashes, she gave him a tremulous smile. She was as nervous as he was. "I'm not sure either. I don't think I have as much experience as you do."

At age forty Jason had been around the block a few times. He'd had serious relationships, casual relationships, and fuck buddies that couldn't even be called relationships. Brinley, on the other hand, was just passed her thirtieth birthday and he doubted she engaged in casual affairs of the heart or body. She was depending on him to take the lead and make things good for both of them. He only hoped he could do just that and not embarrass himself in his haste.

Slow the hell down.

He repeated it a few more times in his head as he tried to even his breathing and calm his racing heart. He knelt on the bed next to her and leaned down so she was trapped between his arms, his palms flat on the mattress.

"Maybe we should start with some kissing and work from there."

"Yes," she breathed, her lips parted and ready. A band wrapped around his heart as he hovered above her, gently exploring her mouth with his own. Softly he ran his tongue across her lower lip before dipping inside to taste her sweetness. Refusing to be hurried, he languidly explored the warm cavern of her mouth before trailing a series of kisses across her jaw and down her neck to a sensitive spot on her shoulder that made her tremble in his arms. Her back arched as his tongue slid to the curve of her breast and her fingers weaved into his hair.

"Jason," she whispered urgently, her legs parting instinctually so he could insinuate himself between her thighs. His hard cock nestled against the warmth of her mound and he rubbed himself against her, making himself crazy with need and sending Brinley into near orgasm. She shuddered against him and wrapped her long, tanned legs around his waist.

"Sweet Brinley," he murmured against the petal soft skin of her breast. His shaking fingers fumbled with the catch on her bra, but thankfully she didn't notice and the material didn't argue. The lacy confection seemed to melt away, revealing dusky pink nipples that were already hard and pointed.

His mouth went dry even as his hands caressed her breasts and pinched the tips, his tongue following right behind. He couldn't get enough of her womanly curves, his fingers tracing the indentation of her waist and the curve of her hip before slipping down to her thighs, taut from gardening and bicycle riding. He tickled her behind the knee before pressing open-mouth kisses down her abdomen, dipping his tongue into her belly button.

Her fingers dug into his shoulders as he ran his tongue under the elastic of her silky panties. Levering up, he hooked his fingers under the waistband and began tugging them slowly down her legs before tossing them away. Completely bare to his gaze, her skin took on a pink hue from her cheeks to her tummy while her hands went up to cover her breasts.

"It's a little late for that now, honey."

Brinley's gaze dropped to her toes and she squirmed on the sheets. "I know. It's just…I'm shy." She looked back up and her lips were trembling. "I know it's silly but I can't help it. Not too many people have seen me…you know…naked."

Jason was heartily grateful to be one of the few who had. Her body was perfect to him and he knew it would take more than one night to learn all its secrets.

"Would it help if I got naked too?"

He'd been too eager to explore her body to take his own clothes off but they needed to go either way. He was finding his jeans too restrictive anyway, almost cutting off his circulation pressing back against his straining cock.

Her hazel eyes went wide and her cheeks turned redder. "Um, that would definitely get my mind off of me."

He backed off the mattress and stood by the bed, tugging at the buttons on his shirt. He shrugged it off before working on his fly, never taking his eyes from her. His mouth went dry when she licked her lips as his cock sprung from the confines of his jeans and boxers. He kicked them away and immediately came back down on the bed with her, capturing those come-hither lips with his own until they were both breathless.

Brinley's arms had snaked around him and her palms were gliding up and down the muscles of his back. His cock was sandwiched between them and he felt the coolness of his precum smeared on his belly. He wouldn't be able to hold back much longer.

It was time to make her fly with pleasure.

✦ ✦ ✦

BRINLEY HAD NEVER felt anything like this before. Innately shy, she found it hard to let go and relax with a man in an intimate situation. Despite being hesitant about her nude body, she'd responded enthusiastically to every kiss and caress. His rough hands felt delicious against her bare skin and she shivered in delight as his fingers found sensitive spots she never knew she had. No man had taken this much time. So patient.

And it looked like he wasn't finished. If he gave her much more pleasure she was going to break into a million little pieces.

But in a really good way.

Jason slid down her body and began tracing patterns on the delicate skin of her inner thigh with his tongue. A strangled moan escaped her lips as a wave of fiery heat swept through her body, sending her arousal into the clouds.

He pushed her legs farther apart and she stiffened when she realized what he intended to do. She'd been the recipient of the most intimate kiss but had never truly enjoyed it. The men had always seemed to be doing it out of guilt rather than want. She didn't want Jason doing it because he had to.

"What's wrong, honey?" Jason's warm breath hovered over her clit, sending frissons of sensation straight to her toes and fingers. "Am I doing something wrong? Just tell me what you want."

Brinley's mind wasn't working clearly enough to even know what she wanted. She did know she wanted to be as close to this man as possible. She wanted to give as well as receive.

The words simply wouldn't come out, getting stuck in her throat.

Lifting her head so she could look into his eyes, she swallowed hard and tried again. "You don't have to...you know. If you don't want to."

Jason looked confused for a moment and then his expression cleared. "If I didn't want to do it I wouldn't. But I do. Very much." He tilted his head, his green eyes soft. "Are we okay? Just relax back and let me take care of you."

Never in her life had she had a man say that to her.

She wasn't about to argue.

Letting her head fall back onto the pillow, she crumpled the sheets in her balled up fists as his tongue began tracing circles around her clit, then down to her opening before traveling back. Her entire body shook with the effort to keep from exploding but Jason wasn't going to let her hold back from him. He was relentless, pressing one, then two fingers inside of her. She was so wet they slid in easily and he hooked them to rub the sweet spot deep within, sending bolts of electricity careening to every corner of her body and mind.

Her brain short-circuited and the room spun as she reached the precipice, her climax turning her world upside down. Glittery lights flashed in front of her eyes as waves of pleasure ran through her like white-water rapids. She rode it until it turned into a gentle stream, her body still floating somewhere in the heavens.

Jason's body lifted from hers, the cool air drying the sheen of sweat on her skin. He rummaged in the nightstand, pulled out a condom square, and then ripped it open with his teeth. Her trembling fingers helped him roll it on his impressive erection before he positioned himself between her thighs. His muscled arms held himself above her and she couldn't stop her own hands from exploring his wide shoulders and ridged abdomen. Her palms slid over the dips and planes of his body as he lowered himself, his steely cock nudging at her entrance.

"We'll take this slow, honey."

His jaw tight with the effort to hold back he pushed forward, paused, and then slowly pressed farther in, letting her stretch to accommodate his girth. Brinley had to catch her breath as he slid in to the hilt, every inch of him filling every nook and cranny of her.

Tingles started deep inside and began to spread through her abdomen, her climb toward orgasm starting all over again. He pulled out and then thrust back in, rods of pleasure shooting through her body and then back to her clit. Each successive stroke sent them both higher until she was clinging to him, the only solid thing in her spinning, topsy-turvy world. Exhortations fell from her lips as she teetered at the edge, needing only a nudge to go over.

Jason buried his face in her neck and his thrusts sped up, each one rubbing against her already sensitive clit. The coil in her belly tightened painfully right before it sprang free and she fell over the edge, her body quivering with the intensity of her climax.

Groaning his own release Jason threw his head back, the veins on his neck standing out in stark relief against his smooth, tanned skin. She ran her hands up and down his back in a soothing motion as he shuddered above her before slumping on top of her, his weight warm and protective.

Eventually he lifted his head, his fingers pushing back her long hair from her face and softly kissed her lips before rolling away. Immediately she missed his warmth and she pulled up the covers while he murmured that he'd be right back. He padded into the ensuite bathroom while she caught her breath, her brain beginning to function once again. By the time he slid in the bed next to her she'd had the opportunity for regrets but didn't feel a single one. She wouldn't have traded this night with Jason for anything in the world.

"Will you sleep in this bed with me tonight?" he asked, his voice soft and low, his breath tickling her ear.

Try and stop her.

"Yes. But shouldn't we let Huck in too?"

She knew the lovable canine liked to crawl into bed with Jason early in the morning.

"He's got you wrapped around his paw. If I let him in he's going to sleep with us," Jason warned, a chuckle in his voice. "Are you sure?"

She was and Jason opened the door. The pup must have heard the latch because he ran into the bedroom, jumped on the mattress, and curled up next to Brinley. She wasn't in any danger but she couldn't have been any safer with Huck on one side and Jason on the other.

"Can you sleep okay?" he asked, scratching Huck behind the

ear. “You’re on his side of the bed so he might get pushy.”

In answer, Brinley scooted closer to Jason and pillowed her head on his shoulder. “Then I hope you don’t mind sharing your half.”

From the look on his face Jason didn’t mind in the least. She cuddled into his large frame and let sleep take over. Tomorrow they’d have to think about the case again but tonight she’d think only of the two of them.

And maybe even let herself imagine…a future.

Chapter Nineteen

"LET ME DO the talking, okay?" Jason asked, giving Brinley a sidelong glance as they pulled into the driveway of Wendell Barnes's home near Bozeman. The house looked remarkably like her own Craftsman home right down to the rockers on the front porch. "Dad gave me a few pointers on talking to him."

"No problem." She climbed down from the truck and took in every detail with a shudder. "This is spooky. Do you see the resemblance?"

Anyone that had seen both houses couldn't miss it. Even the flower beds and bushes were located in the same spots in the front yard.

Fucking weird.

If Wendell Barnes was trying to recreate his life in Tremont he'd done a decent job. It made Jason wonder what the inside looked like.

"Maybe it's a coincidence," Jason said as they tromped up the front porch steps to ring the doorbell. Peter Anderson had called his friend Wendell to ask if he would talk to Jason. They'd received the all clear but Peter had warned his son that Wendell wasn't thrilled about digging up the past and to tread lightly.

The door swung open and a man about the age of Jason's own father stood there. Jason didn't know what he'd been expecting but Wendell was tall with broad shoulders and a square jaw. Despite graying hair and a lined face, the man would still be considered quite handsome.

"You must be Jason Anderson. We met when you were a boy but you probably don't remember it."

Wendell stepped back so they could enter and Jason put his arm around Brinley. "This is Brinley Snow, Mr. Barnes."

They all shook hands and then followed him from the foyer to the living room. Jason and Brinley sat down on the couch while Barnes sat in a chair to their right. Brinley's gaze was darting all around the room, her eyes wide, and Jason knew why. The same as outside, the inside was a mirror image of her own home right down to the built in book shelves in the living room and the mirrored banquet in the dining room. The only difference was the color scheme and Jason knew that Brinley had spent weeks repainting and decorating when she'd moved in.

"So you want to talk about Linda," Wendell began and then looked up when an attractive woman came through from the kitchen with a tray of lemonade. "Ah yes, I asked my wife Lynn to bring us some refreshments. Lynn, this is Jason Anderson and Brinley Snow."

"It's nice to meet you." The dark haired woman sat down and poured four glasses of lemonade and then offered Jason and Brinley a plate of cookies. "Are both of you police officers?"

The shock Jason had felt when seeing Lynn Barnes for the first time was making it difficult to concentrate. There had been a picture of Linda Barnes in the police file he'd gone through. An attractive brunette with a trim figure, she could have been this woman's double.

Spooky as shit. The longer he spent here the stranger it became.

Did Lynn – hell, even the name was almost like Linda's – have any idea she was a dead ringer for Barnes's deceased wife?

A quick glance around the house revealed no family pictures or memorabilia, only two black and white framed photos of the mountains and a lake. But then Barnes wouldn't need photos of the past when he was still living in it.

"I'm actually a police consultant, Mrs. Barnes, and Brinley is a civilian. I just want to thank you for speaking with us today. I'm sure talking about the past is not something you want to do."

Wendell Barnes sniffed in disapproval. "No, it is not. I'd appreciate it if you would ask your questions so we can be done with this." He patted his wife on the hand. "You can ask anything in front of Lynn. She knows the whole story."

"Let's start there then. What do you remember from that night, Mr. Barnes?"

Jason deliberately kept his question open-ended. Guilty suspects tended to start where they felt the most vulnerable instead of at the beginning of the story.

Barnes sat up straight and crossed his arms over his chest, a huge body language give away that he didn't feel like being open and honest. "I suppose you want to know why I was at the lake that night. Well, I'll tell you. Linda and I had an argument and I went for a drive. That's it. Nothing dramatic. Just an ordinary marital spat."

"That's not what you told the police that night," Jason countered, watching the man's expression closely. "You said you were fishing."

Barnes's lips twisted in derision. "I'm no fisherman and the cops knew it. I just knew that if I told them the truth they'd think I'd done it. Hell, they thought it anyway so I needn't have bothered. But I didn't shoot Linda. I loved her."

He loved her so much he'd married her a second time, but with another woman.

"What else do you remember?" Jason prodded. Interesting the first thing Barnes mentioned was his shaky alibi.

"It was an evening like any other." Barnes shrugged carelessly. "We watched some television and that's when we argued. I went out for a drive. I pulled over because I was tired and fell asleep. That's where the police found me. That's all I remember. I told your father I wouldn't be much help."

"You're helping more than you know. Do you have any idea what happened to the gun you owned? It's never been found."

"I hated that gun." The man had a look of distaste that appeared genuine. "I only bought it because we'd been robbed. As for what happened to it, who knows? We had people in and out of the house all the time. Our friends. Workmen. Damian's friends too."

Jason had been able to find out very little about Barnes's progeny. "Your son had friends over quite a bit?"

"All the time. Pretty much every day. You know how kids are."

He sure did and that's why he wanted to talk to Damian

Barnes.

"I'd like to talk to him. Do you have a contact number for him?"

"I can get it but he doesn't know anything. He was out that night." The older man hung his head. "That's my biggest regret. That he found Linda. If I'd come home first it would have been me."

He murmured something to his wife and the woman stood and went into the kitchen for a moment before returning with a business card.

"Here's Damian's contact information. He runs a software company in Billings."

"Thank you, ma'am. I appreciate your help."

Jason tucked the card away in his breast pocket. The police report contained little information from Damian Barnes but there would be no one better to know the true dynamics between Linda and Wendell.

"I doubt he has anything to tell you," Barnes said gruffly. "He was just a boy at the time."

"I'm simply trying to be thorough. I'm planning to speak to your sister-in-law as well."

Barnes laughed humorlessly. "I wasn't Gail's favorite person so I can only imagine what she has to say."

"What is she going to tell me?"

Barnes leaned forward, a grim look on his face. "That Linda and I had a bad marriage which wasn't true at all. All married couples fight. Gail didn't understand that. Last time I saw her she was on her second divorce and counting. She did nothing but complain. Nothing was ever good enough for her. More,

more, more. That's all she cared about. She hated our house, our car, our life and she made sure I knew it every time I saw her. Bitch."

Gail or Linda? Was Barnes conflating the two women? Because it sounded an awful lot like what they'd been told about Wendell's wife.

"One more question. Did you or your wife have any enemies, Mr. Barnes? Someone who might want to hurt your wife or maybe you?"

A sickly grin crossed the man's face and even Lynn Barnes seemed to stiffen in reaction.

"When a man makes money he also makes enemies, although I never took the time to catalog them. Perhaps I should have. Linda might be alive today. As for her, she could be direct and honest which ruffled a few feathers here and there, but no, I don't know of any enemies that would want to hurt her. I'm not sure why the police can't admit that it was a robbery gone bad. That's all. We were supposed to go to a party that night but cancelled at the last minute." Wendell Barnes stood, indicating that the interview was done. "I'm tired of answering the same questions over and over. There was never any evidence that I was guilty. I want to live my life in peace."

In his lookalike house with his doppelgänger wife.

"I'm sorry to have troubled you." Jason and Brinley stood as well. "I hope we don't have to trouble you for another twenty years, Mr. Barnes."

They walked to the front door and Wendell gave them an odd look. "I'm not sure what all the interest is in this now. I told the same thing I told you to that young man."

Jason stopped in his tracks, and pulled his hand from the doorknob. "Young man? Do you remember his name by any chance?"

"Of course I do," Barnes answered briskly. "Roger Gaines. He came here about a month ago asking the very same questions plus a few more. Nosy fellow. He wanted to talk to Damian too."

Barnes knew that Roger was on the trail of his wife's killer. That was motive.

Son of a bitch.

Chapter Twenty

BRINLEY RUBBED THE goosebumps on her arm as they drove away from Wendell Barnes's home. She'd stayed quiet during the interview just as Jason had requested which gave her a front row seat to the myriad of expressions that had crossed his features as he'd answered each question.

The man appeared guilty about his son finding Linda's body but talked about her murder as if discussing the weather. His offhand manner had been shocking to say the least despite the twenty years since the incident. Brinley couldn't help but think that if something happened to Jason talking about it years later would still upset her.

And they weren't even in love. At least she didn't think they were. Her emotions were all mixed up these days and just being near Jason made it hard to think.

"That was one of the creepiest things I've ever seen," she declared, shivering at the memory of Wendell and Lynn Barnes. "She looks just like Linda. They could be sisters."

"Or mother and daughter. I wonder when he met Lynn. I'll have Jared check out her background. If he met her before Linda was shot then that would be another motive, besides money and unhappiness."

"Isn't that enough?"

"It never hurts to see why a criminal is highly motivated to do what they do. Love is a powerful motivator. Honestly, I'm more interested in the fact that he'd met Roger Gaines. He knew he was being investigated again by someone with nothing but free time. Maybe Gaines was getting too close."

"So you think Wendell Barnes is our guy?" The man was weird but Brinley wasn't sure he was a killer, but then she didn't think she'd ever met one.

"He's the best suspect we've got. Right now Jared is digging deep into this guy's finances."

"He didn't have to tell us about Roger Gaines but he did," Brinley pointed out. "There's also the possibility that whomever shot Roger knew all about this investigation. It sounds like he wasn't keeping anything a secret. And the murderer could be using this old case to hide what they've done."

Jared chuckled and pulled into the parking lot of a barbecue joint, putting the truck in park. "You're starting to sound like a cop. So I'll ask you this, Officer Snow. What is your gut telling you?"

Good question. She rooted around in her psyche for a strong feeling one way or the other but couldn't find one. Mostly she was plain confused.

"Right now, nothing. There are too many people that could have shot Roger. His brother, his sister-in-law, even his friend Brad. Could Wendell Barnes have done it? Yes, he gave off a slimy vibe that makes me want to take a shower but that doesn't mean he's a double murderer – triple if you count the attempt on Anita's life. So I pretty much have no idea who killed Linda Barnes. Do you know?"

"No, and I wish I did. But my gut is telling me there's still plenty we don't know and that means we continue to dig for information."

"Where to next?"

The only way to get her life back to normal was to solve this case. Failure? Not an option.

"We're going to have lunch." Jason swung out of the truck and came around to her side to help her down. "Did I mention that Gail was joining us?"

Just once she'd like to be one step ahead of Jason but it was proving impossible. He had some sort of law enforcement mojo that kept him moving forward, plowing through the evidence and uncovering truths.

"You know you didn't." He linked her arm with his and escorted her through the entrance. "I have to admit I'd like to meet her though. She did live in my house for twenty years. I wonder if she'd approve of the changes."

His green eyes were twinkling as he waved to an older woman with silver hair and sensible shoes sitting in a booth about halfway down. "She probably would. Just a word about Gail before you meet her. She's just as Barnes described her – blunt and honest. But what he didn't say was she was a sweet woman who fully embraced life. I think she's a real sweetheart."

"She baked you cookies or something, didn't she?" Brinley asked suspiciously when Jason slid his hand under her elbow to escort her to the table. "You're a sucker for food."

"Gail doesn't bake cookies, I can assure you. She may not

even know what the oven is for."

That explained the pristine condition of the old-fashioned double oven that Brinley adored. It looked like it had barely been used.

The older woman stood and hugged Jason before being introduced to Brinley and shaking her hand. Gail's eyes had lit up when Jason told her that Brinley was the new owner of the house. That had earned Brinley her own hug.

For a woman who had moved into an assisted living apartment Gail looked pretty spry. The hug hadn't been some wimpy, weak thing. She still had some arm strength even at sixty-five. They slid into the booth across from Gail who was drinking an iced tea.

"I hope we haven't kept you waiting. Actually we talked to your brother-in-law this morning."

Jason ordered sodas for himself and Brinley. She flipped open the menu, keeping one eye on the woman who had lived in the house. She'd never met Gail and had only dealt with a broker for the transaction, but this vital woman didn't look much like the house she'd left which had been a haven for cabbage rose wallpaper and chintz draperies.

Gail made a sour face. "Last time I talked to Dell was nineteen and a half years ago when I moved into their old home. He said the place had too many bad memories and he needed a new start."

And then he recreated the entire thing right down to the woman by his side.

"He said you wouldn't have much good to say about him," Brinley responded. "Did you and he not get along?"

"Not in the least," the older woman said bluntly. "He was a miserly, petty, vindictive son of a bitch then and I doubt he's any better now. Richer than God but too cheap to spend a dime of it. He held onto his money with both fists unless it was for that son of his. And that boy was a narcissistic, whiny brat thanks to his father. I told Linda not to marry Dell but she was in love, and you can't reason with that."

"They argued?" Brinley asked, fascinated by the history of her home. "Did it ever get violent?"

Gail snorted as the waitress slid two sodas onto the table. "He didn't have the guts. Never did."

They quickly ordered and the waitress bustled to the next table. Jason leaned forward, his gaze intent on their guest.

"So you don't think Wendell killed Gail?"

"As much as I didn't like the selfish little weasel I don't think he murdered her. He needed her to keep up the fiction of a happy family to the outside world." Gail's lips twisted in distaste. "My fear is that my sister's own actions got her killed. You see, Linda was known to do stupid, harebrained things. God made her pretty but he didn't make her smart."

Brinley wasn't sure how to take that statement. "I'm not sure what you mean, Mrs. Denton."

"Call me Gail." The woman waved her hand. "What I mean is that Linda had the looks but was dumb as a rock. Is that plain enough for you? She was my sister and I loved her, but I was not unaware of her shortcomings and I'm sure she could have cataloged all of mine as well. Linda lacked common sense and often had to be rescued from situations. That's how she met Wendell. Do you have family like that?"

A picture of Dawn floated through Brinley's mind but she dashed it away quickly. Dawn wasn't stupid, just a trifle self-absorbed. Oblivious to what went on outside her bubble of a world. But she had a loving heart and cared about her family and friends even if she didn't always notice what was going on in their lives.

"I'm afraid I don't. What kind of situations are you talking about?"

"Men. Lots of them." Gail took a sip of her iced tea and then slapped down the glass. "Linda was constantly leading men on and then shocked when they expected something. I imagine that's what ended her life."

"A disgruntled suitor?" Jason queried. "Did you tell the police this?"

Gail rolled her eyes. "Yes, but they were only interested in Wendell."

It was a telling point that despite Gail's animosity toward her ex-brother-in-law that she didn't think him capable of murder.

"Do you have any names?" Jason reached into his breast pocket for his small notebook and pencil but Gail was shaking her head. "I'm afraid not. At that point we weren't spending much time together since I didn't get along with Dell."

More hopes dashed away. Jason was right when he said they'd take two steps forward and one step back constantly during an investigation. Being a cop had to be full of frustration.

"But he gave you the house," Brinley pointed out. "If you two didn't like each other why would he do that?"

"I was in the process of divorcing my second husband and I think Dell was afraid I'd try and claim some of Linda's property.

She wasn't destitute when she met Dell and she had jewelry and money of her own. He wanted to keep it and I needed a place to live so he offered me the house. I only took it to spite him but found that I liked living there. Until recently, of course. I hope you're enjoying it."

"It didn't bother you that your sister had been murdered there?" Brinley asked. No one on the planet could convince her to live in a house where her sister had been shot and killed.

"No, but I'm a practical person who needed a place to live. I concentrated on making it my own rather than thinking about how Linda had lived and died there. Are you making changes to the house? I expect you want to update it quite a bit."

Oh yes.

"I've pulled down all the wallpaper and tore up the carpeting. I finished painting the walls and the cabinets last week. Next are new floors. I'm hoping I can get away with just refinishing them but I think some spots are going to need to be replaced." Brinley bit her lip in worry. "Does it bother you to hear about changes being made in your home?"

"As I said I'm not that sentimental." Gail shook her head and reached across the table to pat Brinley's hand. "Not to worry, dear. It's your home now and you should do whatever you wish. I'm just sorry we didn't meet before, but then the real estate agent handled the sale for me."

"Me too."

Although Brinley didn't completely understand the older woman she did like her. Her blunt, no nonsense attitude was a nice change from so many people that Brinley had met in her life.

"I have one more question, Gail, if you don't mind. Did you ever suspect Wendell of cheating?" Jason asked. "Specifically, was there a woman named Lynn? Someone who looked very much like Linda?"

"No, why do you ask?"

"When we talked to Wendell we found he had remarried. The woman's name was Lynn and she could have been Linda's sister. The house also looked exactly the same," Brinley explained, glancing at Jason.

Gail was frowning, her brow scrunched in thought. "I'm not surprised he remarried, if only for the sake of the boy. As for things looking exactly the same, well, Dell was always an odd bird. But you don't understand things if you think he was trying to recreate his life with Linda. He didn't love her like that. He married my sister because she looked like his first wife, Donna. But of course Linda wasn't and he never forgave her for that."

One more reason for Wendell Barnes to be guilty as hell.

Chapter Twenty-One

"SO YOU THINK Barnes did it?" Logan asked when they were all together again that evening. Brinley and Jason had picked up pizza on the way home and they were all sharing what they'd learned that day while relaxing at Jason's dinner table.

"His alibi sucks," Jason said bluntly. "If he resented Linda for not being his first wife and their marital problems were real then he has the most motive."

Brinley slid another slice onto her plate. "What about Linda's boyfriends? Gail said that her sister was always leading men on. I can see where that would piss someone off."

"Enough to kill?" Jason rubbed his chin. "I'm not sure about that. Besides, there's nothing in the police file about any boyfriend and they talked to all the couple's friends. Surely a girlfriend would have said something."

Logan grinned and popped open a soda can. "I'm with Jason on this one. But then I've seen what Jared emailed over earlier today."

"You better have the evidence to back up that look," Jason warned, shaking a slice at Logan. "What did he send over?"

Logan reached behind him and dropped a file in the middle

of the table. "Fascinating reading. Take a look at the photos of wife number one and two. They could be twins."

Jason flipped open the folder and placed it between himself and Brinley. He wiped his hands on a napkin before piecing through the file. Near the top was a family photo of Wendell, his first wife, and their young son Damian who at the time was probably eight or nine years old. The smiles on their faces looked genuine but Jason knew from his law enforcement days that it could all be an elaborate facade. Underneath could have been rotten to the core.

Brinley pointed to the son. "Poor little guy. I bet the kids were really mean to him. I see that every day at school."

Wendell's son appeared to be the stereotypical geek. Thin and small, the blond haired tyke wore thick black-framed glasses along with a plaid vest and a bow tie. If any of his friends saw him in that outfit there was no way the little boy wasn't going to be teased about it. Add in the fact Damian looked scrawny and small for his age and Jason felt for the kid. He'd probably had a terrible time with bullies.

"Did Jared have any luck finding Damian? I texted him the phone number that Barnes gave me." Jason paged through the file to see if there were any later photos of the family but came up empty. "I would very much like to talk to the son."

Logan shook his head. "He got the secretary so he left a message. Then he hunted down the house phone number and left a message there. Hopefully this Damian Barnes will call back tonight or tomorrow."

"Here's the pictures side by side." Brinley set the photo of Linda next to the family photo. "They do look creepily alike."

"It's not uncommon for a man to have a type." Logan tapped on the picture. "Some men only like blondes. Some only like redheads. I'm not sure you can call a man guilty because he keeps marrying women who look like each other. Now the house thing, that is strange. I don't know any man who ever gave a shit how his home was decorated. When Ava moved in she put up valances. Hell, I didn't even know what they were. They look nice and all but I could have gone my entire life never having them. Most men feel the same."

Brinley's gaze flickered to Jason's back window and smirked. He had blinds on every window but the only drapes were in the bedroom where he wanted it dark in case he needed to sleep during the day.

"That's not the most interesting thing though." Logan shuffled the papers and pulled out one. "The financial stuff is what got to me. Wendell Barnes raked in some big bucks when Linda died. He had her insured for two hundred thousand."

For the first time that day Jason felt like there was light at the end of the proverbial tunnel. "Finally a goddamn motive that makes sense. How did the police not know this? This wasn't in the case file."

"I can answer that." West stood in the doorway, looking tired and pissed off. "I just went three rounds with the mayor. I asked him about that day that he argued with Barnes. Turns out Barnes had lost a bet to Cavendish and didn't want to pay up."

"That doesn't answer why it wasn't in the police file." Brinley stood and retrieved another plate from the cabinet along with a can of soda from the refrigerator. "Have a seat. There's plenty of pizza and breadsticks."

"And I can answer that." Jason scooted his chair over to make room for West. "Canvendish and Barnes were pretty big deals in this town and had a lot of friends. They could make sure nothing appeared in the official file."

"Small town hide and seek." Logan smiled but it was more grim than happy. "I know it well. You should have seen the mess I inherited when I became sheriff."

"That's Cavendish's legacy." West slapped down the can so hard soda flew from the top and landed on his hand and the table. "Corruption and back room deals. We need someone to come in and clean up this town."

West reached behind and grabbed a towel from the kitchen counter to mop up the mess he'd made. Jason was grinning from ear to ear and Brinley didn't have a clue as to why he was so darn happy. This entire case was a mess.

"You're grinning like the village idiot, brother. What's so wonderful?" West tossed the towel back on the counter before digging back in to his dinner.

"You." Jason pointed a finger at his brother with a laugh. "You talk like there's some magical being that's going to rush in and sweep away all the crap that's been building up here in Tremont for the last twenty years. You're deliberately overlooking the obvious."

"It's not obvious to me but then I just moved here. What are you talking about?" Brinley's gaze went to Jason then West, then Jason again trying to figure out what was going on between these two brothers. Even Logan was wearing a scowl and he was usually smiling.

"Aww, hell," West muttered. "No way. I know what you're

thinking and it's not going to happen. I have a job."

"So? Cavendish did as well before becoming mayor. You should run. You'd do a good job."

Brinley's eyes went wide. "West run for Mayor? He'd get my vote."

"See? You already have a vote." Jason balled up his napkin and tossed it at his morose brother.

"What? You won't vote for me? If you do and Brinley does and I do, hell, that's three votes. At least I wouldn't be completely shut out."

West wasn't taking this seriously but Jason was warming to the idea.

"I'm sure Mom and Dad will vote for you. Maybe our sister too. That's six." Jason jumped to his feet, his mind going a mile a minute. "Dad's got a lot of friends that can help you. Donate to the campaign and all that. Let's face it. No one really likes Leon. He only won last time because the other guy was even sleazier. Give the people an honest choice and you'll win by a landslide."

"That's what I'm afraid of," barked West. "If you think it's such a great idea you do it."

"I'm busy getting my business off the ground. You should think about this," Jason urged. "You complain about Cavendish nonstop and everyone else does too. If you don't like him, do something about it."

West looked like he wanted to punch Jason but to his credit all he did was groan and slump in his chair. "I hate it when you're right. Leon has to go but there has to be another way."

"If you can think of another way, I'm all for it. But I think we both know that unseating him is what needs to happen."

West picked up the pizza slice. "No more talking about running for mayor. We have a murder to solve. No, make that two murders. Tell me everything about your day. I'm hoping we're getting close."

"Something is going to give and soon," Jason promised. "The insurance money is a huge clue. Wendell Barnes is starting to look good for it."

But even if Barnes killed Linda, did that mean he automatically killed Gaines and shot Anita Hazlitt? Jason believed the two cases were entwined but he had to prove it. And that wasn't going to be easy.

Chapter Twenty-Two

BRINLEY ROUSED FROM a deep sleep, rubbing her eyes and groaning at the luminous numbers on the clock. Two in the damn morning.

Yawning widely, she levered up on her elbows and listened for a long moment, trying to figure out what had woken her at this ungodly hour of the night. A low moan pierced the silence and one look a Jason told her he was in the midst of a nasty nightmare.

At some point he'd kicked the covers off, although he'd twisted the top sheet around his legs and appeared to be trying desperately to free them. His arm flailed and missed her head by inches as he gasped, barely intelligible words falling from his lips.

She could make out "no" but that was about it.

"Jason." Brinley tentatively touched his shoulder, his skin damp with sweat. "Jason, wake up."

He frowned and shook his head, another moan that sounded like it was dragged from somewhere deep inside of him.

"Jason," she said, louder and more firmly this time. "It's Brinley. Everything is fine. Wake up for me. Everything is okay. You're okay."

His lids fluttered and then he sat straight up, his arms shooting out and knocking her to the mattress while he dragged air into his lungs. His gaze darted around the room as if to assess his whereabouts before he groaned and buried his face in his hands, his body trembling.

Whatever terrible nightmare he'd been having was probably the reason he didn't sleep well or all that much. She reached out once more and placed her arm around his shoulders, cuddling close until he stopped shaking and finally looked up and into her eyes.

"Jesus, I never wanted you to see that."

His voice sounded hoarse and she wanted to get him a drink of water but she couldn't leave him in this state. Rubbing her hands up and down his arms in a soothing motion, she pressed a kiss to his bare shoulder.

"You were dreaming."

Jason shook his head and sighed. "Honey, that's the last thing it was. There was nothing remotely pleasant. I was having a nightmare. The one tonight is apparently my subconscious's favorite. I get it at least once every couple of weeks."

Her fingers ran down his back, feeling the ridged scars of his ordeal. She'd felt them the first night they'd been together but hadn't known what to say. Or if she should say anything at all. She couldn't even begin to understand what he'd been through but she was here…and she heal him in any way she could.

"Tell me about it," she offered softly, wanting dearly to take away this man's pain but not having a clue as to how. "It might help."

He gave her a lopsided smile. "Sure. It might help give you

nightmares. It's so ugly, honey. I don't want this to touch you in any way."

Men were so silly sometimes, always trying to protect the frail woman from things they didn't need to be shielded from in the first place.

"It already has." She set her chin on his shoulder and pulled him closer. "Please tell me. I want to help you."

Jason didn't say anything and the silence stretched on as they sat on the bed huddled together. Finally he sat back, propped against the headboard so she could lay her head on his chest. His heart galloped underneath her ear, telling her in no uncertain terms that whatever haunted him at night was truly evil.

"They tortured me."

His voice was a mere whisper in the darkness. She stayed perfectly still and quiet, letting him gather his thoughts and emotions. It humbled her beyond words that he would bare his soul to her this way, and if it was possible it made her fall for him all the harder that he could allow himself to be this vulnerable in her company.

"They used whips and white-hot irons. Sometimes electricity. There was pain every day. In a way you get used to it so they have to ramp it up each time until you're closer and closer to death at the end of each session. I'd sometimes pray for death to take me. Then afterward I'd feel guilty that I'd been so weak."

Brinley's fingers tightened on Jason's bicep but she steeled herself not to react to the horror unfolding with each passing moment. Pressing her lips together, she suppressed the words that wouldn't make any difference and only minimize what he'd been through. There was nothing she could say to wipe away the terror like tears on a three-year old's face. No platitudes that would make this go away, shelving neatly somewhere in a closet called "the past."

"The first few times you're so proud of yourself for not screaming like the others, but then after several days your defenses are broken down one by one and you realize the screaming in your ears is your own. You know in that moment that you're not as strong as you think you are. That nothing you've been trained for is going to save your ass. That's when reality hits you and you face the fact that you're going to die there and then be thrown out like a piece of garbage. There was no sanctity to life. People died for something as minor as being friends with the wrong person. No one gave a shit about anything but money and power."

Wiping a silent tear from her face, she listened to his pain filled voice and tried to hold him more closely as if she could shield him from something. Maybe herself. She had torn at this scab and it hit her she might have only made things worse. Much worse.

She couldn't bear the thought she might have hurt this man she cared so deeply for.

Was it love? She didn't know, although he was more than deserving of the emotion. Anyone who had survived what he had and could still care about others was worthy of all the love and devotion she could give.

"You don't have to–" she began but he pressed his fingers to her lips.

"You were right. Holding it in hasn't helped. Maybe talking about it will. You need to know just how fucked up I am. I don't know if I'll ever get any better. I may be this fucking broken for the rest of my life. You sure as hell deserve better."

"You're not broken," she protested but he simply shook his head, his gaze far away somewhere. He was back there and she damned her stupidity for asking him to relive this. She'd been arrogant and smug thinking she knew what to do to help him. She didn't know anything and now she could only hold him to keep the nightmares at bay. She wished she could take the pain away that she knew dogged him every night but she didn't have a clue as to how.

"One day the guard came to my cell and took me outside, which they hadn't done before. I thought maybe it was my chance to escape. Maybe they were transferring me to another prison. But that's not what that day was about."

A chill ran down her spine, tension building at his ominous statement. What he was about to tell her was what he'd been reliving tonight while he slept. She knew it without him having to say it out loud.

"They tied my hands behind me and pushed my back up against a wall. There were several men with guns about ten feet away and they were all smiling and laughing. One yelled at me asking what my last request was. It was then I realized they were going to execute me. A firing squad. It's funny after praying for death to take me I suddenly didn't want to die. I wanted to live very much and see my family and friends again. I wanted to eat pizza and drink a beer. I wanted to feel the joy of sex and the warmth of laughter. I hadn't really lived at all. I had just worked all that time and I had so many goddamn regrets at that moment."

Her throat was swollen shut with emotion, and instead of speaking she planted light kisses on his chest along with a few tears.

"No crying, honey." He lifted her chin so she was looking into his green eyes that were now a stormy gray. "I'm here and selfishly telling you this story. Laying all my baggage at your feet."

"I asked you to," she croaked, barely getting the words out. "It's not selfish."

"It's not smart," he countered. "Now you're going to feel sorry for me. It might sound stupid but a man wants a woman to look up to him. Admire him. He wants her to believe she can depend on him. You probably think I'm a wreck and I guess I am."

Brinley sat straight up and cupped his face in her hands. "I do admire you. And I know I can depend on you. You've protected me, Jason. I've never felt as safe in my life as I do with you."

He snatched her into his arms, and she reveled in the power he held so carefully in check. He was a man who could kill or maim but he chose to be gentle.

Jason sighed and loosened his grip, dropping a kiss on the top of her head. "They put a blindfold on me and made me stand there. I heard them getting ready to shoot and then the sound of guns firing. I fell to my knees. I'd thought I'd died but it was a mock execution. They jerked the blindfold off of me and they were all laughing. They'd shot in another direction. But the guard that took me back to my cell said the next day it would be real. Or maybe not. That I would never know when the real thing was going to happen."

"How many times?" she asked, stroking his face, his cheek stubbly under her palm. "The cruelty of that is unthinkable. Did they do this to everyone?"

"Yes, it was how they amused themselves. They did it three more times but I think the next one was going to be real, because Selena came to me the next day and gave me the information that allowed me to escape."

Someday Brinley wanted to thank that woman who had risked her own life for a man she barely knew.

"Weren't you afraid you'd get caught?"

"I was more afraid of staying. I was definitely going to die there if I didn't try. At least if I was shot dead trying to escape it would be quick."

She couldn't wrap her mind around preferring a quick death to something far more painful. Jason had been through so much and yet he was still strong, facing life head on.

"I don't know what to say after hearing that," she admitted. "I knew it was something awful and it was. I guess I would say that you must be an incredibly strong person to have survived that and come out the other side. I don't think I could have."

"The instinct to survive is overwhelming. Don't underestimate what you might be capable of if you're put into a dangerous situation. I'm not that special."

"I think you're special," she said deeply, brushing his lips with her own as her heart squeezed painfully. The emotions he aroused were stronger than anything she'd known before. "The most special man I've ever known in my life."

His arms tightened around her. "I think you're pretty damn

special too. After reliving near death I want to feel alive. With you. The way I feel with you is exactly what I dreamed about in that prison. I want to make love with you, Brinley."

✦ ✦ ✦

JASON GENTLY PRESSED his lips to Brinley's, overcome with desire, tenderness, and pure emotion for this woman whose mere touch seemed to make everything better. He'd admitted his great flaw, his broken psyche but instead of pushing him away in self-preservation she'd wrapped her arms around him tighter, not scared of him pulling her down with him. He ought to get the hell out of her life when this case was over but damned if he could even fathom the possibility.

He wanted her too badly.

"Jason," she whispered against his skin as she pressed her lips to his shoulder. She shuddered underneath him as his hands roamed over her curves urgently, barely able to rein in his impatience. He needed to be inside of her. Now.

"Yes, honey. I know what you need."

Her own fingers were exploring the ridges of his stomach before slipping down to encircle his hard and ready cock. Jason buried his face in her neck, breathing in the delicate scent of her skin as he kissed and licked a trail to her shoulder, shoving her oversized nightshirt aside to reveal her golden sun-kissed flesh.

Hurriedly he tugged the cotton material over her head and tossed it aside, not caring where it landed. Her lacy panties were next to nothing, barely any covering at all but he wanted nothing between them tonight. All of his own armor had been stripped away with her tender questioning and he was laid bare – body and soul. In the morning he'd have to rebuild it but for now it was a relief to shake it off.

Groaning as her hands caressed his cock, he cupped her breasts in his palms before lapping at a nipple with his tongue bringing it to a hard point. He moved to the other, licking and worrying it with his teeth until it sat up tight and proud in pink perfection.

The pressure was already beginning to build in his lower back, the tide battering at the door. Her own movements were frantic as she wriggled underneath him, rubbing her silky soft skin against him and sending frissons of electricity straight to his balls and cock.

Sliding his hand between her legs, he carefully pressed a finger inside her to test her readiness. Hot and wet, her body wrapped around his flesh and he added another digit to rub her sweet spot while his thumb brushed her clit.

"Yes, oh yes," she moaned, her head thrown back and her eyes half-closed in ecstasy. She was trembling on the brink; he could feel it as her inner walls fluttered around his hand. He withdrew his fingers and reached for the nightstand drawer, fumbling until he found a condom square.

Clumsy in his haste, he ripped open the package and rolled on the protection. Brinley tried to help but it only made it more difficult with every brush of her hands against his already sensitized flesh. Fire licked his skin and his breathing was ragged as he hovered above Brinley, his gaze taking in every inch of the delicious feast before him.

Her long brown hair was tousled around her head like a halo, a few strands hanging down playing hide and seek with her flushed nipples. Her chest rose and fell quickly, her own breathing ragged even as she paused to allow him to look his fill of her beauty. One of his hands skimmed down her side, tracing the indentation of her waist, the gentle flare of her hip, and the long line of her legs, firm from riding her bicycle. He wanted to spend hours drinking in every minute detail…

But not at this moment. He was too needy and from the restless movements she made Brinley felt exactly the same.

"Are you ready for me?" His hoarsely voiced question was met with an eagerness that made his chest tighten. She deserved better and the right thing to do would be to walk away. Let her find someone less damaged, someone who didn't dread the long, dark nights.

"Yes. Now." Her fingernails dug into the muscles of his shoulders and he lowered himself between her legs until his cock lined up with her entrance.

Leaning forward, he captured her full lips with his own even as he surged into her with one stroke. So wet and ready for him, he slid in easily and paused to savor the feeling when he was in to the hilt, her channel walls tightly hugging his cock. He had to close his eyes and think cold thoughts to be able to hold back.

Politics. Ranch bookkeeping. Golf scores. Government expense reports.

Dry, bland topics kept him from embarrassing himself but it had been too close for comfort. This woman was hell on any sense of equilibrium.

Slowly he pulled almost all the way out before thrusting back in, tingles shooting from the top of his head to the tip of his toes and settling in his groin, making it damn hard to think clearly—if at all. Brinley's hips swiveled as he repeated the movement and he had to choke back a groan of pleasure so acute it was painful. Her fingers dug into his biceps as he sped up, pistoning in and out of her until both of them reached the pinnacle.

Brinley cried out his name as she tumbled over the cliff, her sex clamping down on his cock and making it impossible for him to hold back any longer. Stars whirled in front of his eyes as he dragged air into his starved lungs. The pressure in his balls gave way and his seed jetted into the condom. It seemed to go on forever but then finally he was done, wrung out. He rolled over onto his back, carrying Brinley with him and cuddling her damp body close until he was forced to take his leave for a few minutes.

When he returned he slid next to her on the cool sheets, their bodies still overheated from the passion they'd shared. Jason combed back a few stray strands of hair from her face and dropped a brief kiss on her lips.

"It just gets better and better," she sighed, wriggling until her head was pillowed on her shoulder. "I don't know any other word but *wow.*"

Jason chuckled, not at her inarticulate verbal skills but because he completely agreed. There wasn't an adjective for the incredibly amazing hot sex…except *incredible amazing hot sex.*

And somehow it didn't seem enough. Too weak.

"Wow is right. You pack a wallop, honey."

She balanced on her elbow so she could look into his eyes and poked a finger in his chest.

"I could say the same for you. I don't think I could sleep after that. Do you want to watch some television or something?"

So sweet and caring but he was on to her. She knew he wouldn't be able to sleep after the nightmare he'd had but she didn't want him to feel badly about it.

"I'm not sure there's much on but we could look for a movie or something," he agreed. "It will be morning in a couple of hours."

He reached for the remote but kept one arm around Brinley. He'd have to let her go at some point. It would be selfish to keep her but right now she was all his. He would hold on to her for as long as he dared.

Chapter Twenty-Three

"I'LL BE FINE here with Logan. Go on," Brinley urged Jason a few days later over breakfast. "You can tell me about your meeting with Damian Barnes when you get back."

"Possible meeting," Jason corrected, helping himself to another waffle and smothering it in syrup. "He hasn't returned my messages so I'm just going to take a chance and drive to his home and try to corner him. I imagine this is a subject he's not eager to discuss with me—or anyone else, for that matter."

"Poor bastard found the body. That will change a person." Logan leaned against the kitchen counter and refilled his coffee cup. He'd been spending his nights at Brinley's house to make sure no one broke in but during the day he could keep an eye on it from a distance if needed. "What will we be doing today, Miss Snow? Painting? Wallpaper? No, wait…maybe ceiling fans?"

Logan had that boyish grin on his face so clearly he wasn't worried. He'd spent the last couple of days helping her hang ceiling fans and replacing the kitchen backsplash with copper tiles. In fact, she'd been surprised to find how handy he was around the house and he didn't complain a bit about his babysitting job, whether it was her or the house he was watching.

She had to admire his "embrace each day and laugh about it" attitude.

"Nothing that interesting, I'm afraid. We're going to take a break today. I have to meet the flooring company this morning. They're coming to measure and give me an estimate for refinishing the hardwood. Then I need to go to the grocery store because we're out of almost everything, unless you two want to eat cereal for dinner tonight."

Both men vigorously shook their heads. Jason and Logan had healthy appetites and frankly so did she. It didn't hurt that they raved about everything she cooked, whether it was as simple as waffles or as complex as a chocolate soufflé.

"So it's a day of rest? I can live with that. We can go see a movie or something if Jason isn't back yet."

Jason tossed the newspaper aside. "If I can't find Barnes I won't be gone long. This case has come to a grinding halt. Anita didn't see who shot her and we have no new evidence. Just a bunch of theories we can't prove."

She'd been thinking about that very thing last night as Jason had finally fallen asleep around midnight. The fact was she couldn't live here forever. No matter how nice that sounded. Jason hadn't said anything these last few days but the question of what they were going to do about her living arrangements was going to rear its ugly head eventually. They couldn't go on as they were now. At some point she was going to have to suck it up and move back to her house whether it was dangerous or not.

"I've been thinking about that. Maybe I should move back to my house as a sort of bait. My presence there might bring out whoever broke in and lead us to the killer if they're not one and the same person."

"No," Logan and Jason practically shouted in unison. Jason looked horrified at the suggestion and even the laid back Logan appeared alarmed.

"I don't think we're desperate enough to use an innocent young woman as bait for a multiple murderer. Holy hell, woman, that's the craziest idea I've ever heard." Jason slapped his forehead and stood so he was hovering over her. "We will solve this eventually but we don't need to put you in harm's way to do it."

"It was just an idea," she replied weakly. "I can't stay here forever. No one solved the original murder. What if you can't get him again?"

Jason looked so affronted she immediately wanted to take her words back. "I always get my man, Brinley. I realize you're not familiar with my body of work but I dig until I find what I'm looking for. I can assure you Logan and Jared are the same. We'll get him. I'm sorry that you can't stay in your own home, but until we know what's going on here I just can't take any chances."

Before she could apologize he'd slapped his cowboy hat on his head and snatched up his keys from the counter. He was striding out the door when she finally found her voice.

"Jason, wait a minute."

"Got to go." He didn't turn back but he did pause. "I'll call later and let you know how it's going."

He headed out the door but this time she was ready for it. She grabbed his arm just as he hit the bottom front porch step.

"Please wait." She tugged at his shirt until he looked at her.

The hurt she saw in his eyes almost took her breath away. She'd insulted him and she hadn't meant to. "Listen, I'm really sorry. I've got a big mouth and I let it run this morning. I know you're going to catch this guy. You're so close. I just feel like I'm imposing by staying with you. I'm sure you like your privacy and now I've got makeup crap all over your bathroom."

✦ ✦ ✦

BRINLEY HAD NO earthly idea why Jason was really upset and that was probably a good thing. When she'd started talking about going back to her own house, Jason's heart had skipped a beat or two in his chest. He didn't want her to go. He liked having her things strewn through his house. Before she'd come into his life his home had been quiet but sterile. Now it was full of life and he had her to thank for that. Her clothes and mascara didn't seem like a big deal when the remedy meant he'd be alone. Again.

But she thought he was upset that she'd wondered aloud whether he was going to be able to solve the murders.

That didn't bother him in the least. Hell, he'd been wondering the same goddamn thing for days so he couldn't blame her for doing it too. He couldn't guarantee success although he had a track record that other agents envied. He'd do his best, but in the end sometimes these things had an element of luck to them.

So was he lucky if he didn't solve the murder and she stayed? Or was he lucky if he found the killer and she went back to her own house?

He didn't have a fucking clue except that he couldn't be in

this for the long haul. She deserved a better man. A whole man, and that left him out of the running. He hadn't expected to fall so far, so fast. He never had before. Brinley had changed more than she knew.

"It's fine. You didn't say anything wrong. I'm shooting off my mouth too, acting like I know for sure I'm going to solve it when I really don't."

He could see the doubt in her eyes and didn't have a clue how to make it go away. He didn't like lying to her much either.

"My words were thoughtless and I'm so sorry, Jason. Please forgive me."

Brinley squeezed his arm, her eyes beseeching him. Dammit. He'd forgive her damn near anything. He couldn't let her feel like crap when it wasn't her fault. They needed to talk about this sooner or later, although he'd been hoping for the latter.

"That wasn't why I was upset," he admitted. "It was when you talked about moving back to your house. I like having you near me. I don't mind your stuff at all."

A slow smile crossed her pretty face. "Not even the clutter in the shower? I have shampoo, two kinds of conditioner, a soap for my body, one for my face, a razor, and body exfoliator."

"Don't forget that stone that you use to smooth your feet," Jason laughed. "And no, I don't mind. I'm kind of fascinated by it all, actually. I had a sister, but we didn't share a bathroom so I didn't know what half that stuff was until you told me."

He'd asked her about the stone that sat on the edge of the tub after wracking his brain trying to figure out what the hell it was. The only thing he could come up with was a weapon to throw at someone's head if they intruded on her bath time.

"I just didn't want to be in the way. In your way, I mean."

"You could never be that. I'd let you stay just for your cooking alone. But we probably need to have a talk about things eventually. About what happens when this is all over."

"That sounds ominous." Her smile wavered slightly. "Am I going to be thrown out of the Homeowner's Association?"

"No way." Jason leaned down and pressed a kiss to her tempting lips. She tasted like coffee and maple syrup. "But things will change at some point. We don't need to talk about it now though. Tomorrow or the next day is soon enough. Have fun with Logan today. I'll call you later this morning, okay?"

"Okay, drive careful."

Jason climbed into his truck, his gaze still on Brinley standing on the steps, an uncertain expression on her face. He'd fucked this up royally but he'd make it right. This was about his deficiencies, not hers.

He waved as he headed down the road. It was time to get back to the one thing he knew how to do.

Find a criminal.

Chapter Twenty-Four

"JASON'S RUNNING SCARED, isn't he?"

Brinley and Logan had spent the last hour debating the merits of blinds versus shutters and were now sitting at her kitchen table as two men from the flooring company measured each room and scratched the number down on a clipboard. They'd already finished the upstairs and only had the living and dining areas left to do.

"Yes," she sighed in resignation. "He's pulling away from me and I can't stop him. Maybe it's for the best if he really doesn't want me."

"He wants you," Logan laughed. "Trust me, he does. He's just confused. Kind of like my mom used to say. He doesn't know whether to scratch his watch or wind his butt. You've got him all turned around and he's going to go down fighting."

Logan's poetic way with words had her laughing right along with him. "What if he doesn't get himself straightened out? Maybe I should help him."

"Jason is a hell of a lot like I was, darlin'. Love and commitment snuck up on me. Sure, I fought it, but Ava just quietly hung around and waited for me to remove my head from my ass.

No pushing. No yelling. She just carried on with life as if I was smart enough to figure it out on my own. And I did. Jason will too. Give him love and space and he'll figure out he wants a bunch of the former and none of the latter."

She hoped so because her feelings deepened with every day that she spent with him.

"I'll try and relax. No worrying over tomorrow."

"What Jason is going through – and what I went through – didn't have a damn thing to do with a female. This is about Jason's demons, Brinley, and only he can fight them."

Logan was right but it wasn't easy to sit back and pretend not to care about the outcome. She cared more than she was ready to admit.

A banging on the front door interrupted them and she apologized and excused herself to answer it, leaving Logan to finish his coffee. She pulled open the door and almost slammed it closed immediately.

It was Greg. He wasn't giving up. What did it take for the guy to get a clue? She didn't want to be a bitch but he couldn't keep showing up here uninvited. And unwanted.

"Hey, Brinley. How have you been?"

Greg's charming smile did nothing to soothe her ruffled feathers. His habit of showing up out of the blue and trying to charm her was wearing on her nerves. She kept the screen door shut between them, not wanting him to think there was a chance in hell she was going to ask him inside the house.

"What do you want, Greg?"

She didn't bother to temper the annoyance in her voice and her mother would have told her she sounded rude. Good.

Apparently Greg was the kind of guy who needed a brick wall to fall on him before he realized what was going on around him.

That smile she once thought was charming but now just seemed smarmy crossed his pretty boy face. She didn't know how she ever could have been attracted to him or his type. Jason was a million times more handsome and sexy with his rugged looks and godlike physique.

"I was passing by and thought we might visit for awhile. Maybe have a cup of coffee and talk. You know, catch up."

"No." Brinley shook her head, her lips pressed tightly together. "I told you the last time I saw you that this is not going to work out. You need to leave."

"Trouble, Brinley?"

A deep voice right behind her had a look of dismay crossing Greg's face. Logan stood to her right but even Greg could see the wide shoulders and powerful muscles on the former sheriff. It wasn't even a question who would come out on top if there was a scuffle.

"He was just leaving, Logan. Right, Greg?"

Red-faced, Greg took a step back on the porch. "If that's how you really feel then I will go."

"Do that. It's not going to work out. I'm sorry."

She wasn't all that sorry really but she was sorry that she was having to deal with this again. The whole situation creeped her out, and that was saying something after what had happened to her in Chicago.

Greg turned on his heels and strode to his non-descript sedan, climbing in and gunning the engine. Dirt flew behind the wheels as he backed out of the driveway and onto the main road.

Brinley turned to Logan who was wearing a sour expression as he watched the other man hightail it out of there.

"Thank you. I could have gotten rid of him eventually but you being here made it much easier."

Brinley closed the door and took another peek out of the front window to ensure Greg was gone. "Who is that and what's his deal? I know first impressions don't count for much, but I think he's an asshole."

Laughter bubbled from her lips at Logan's bald statement. "Greg is an asshole. He's a guy I kind of dated. Coffee dates and stuff like that. Apparently he doesn't like the word no."

"Greg, huh? I hope he keeps his damn distance from now on or Jason and I might have to have a chat with him. Man to man. Some guys just don't get the whole 'no means no' thing. I know because I put more than a few of them in jail."

"He's harmless. But a nuisance. He keeps showing up uninvited. I have to admit that's a hot button issue with me."

"I'll keep an eye out for Romeo." Logan crossed his arms over his chest, his blue eyes like ice. "The flooring guys are finished, by the way, and waiting for you in the kitchen. I gave them some coffee. I hope that's okay."

"Perfect. Now cross your fingers that their estimate to refinish these floors isn't an arm and a leg. I've only budgeted for one limb. Two is out of the question."

Shaking off her anger and frustration, Brinley crossed into the kitchen. It was sadly ironic that Greg wouldn't leave her alone and Jason was looking for reasons to bolt.

All she needed to do was make sure she didn't give him any reason to do so.

✦ ✦ ✦

JASON ENTERED THE elevator and punched the "4" button on the panel. He'd struck out at Damian Barnes's home. There'd been no one at the house and the place looked deserted with a pile of newspapers on the front porch. So now Jason was giving Barnes's workplace a try but wasn't optimistic about his chances of meeting the elusive man.

The doors slid open and Jason walked down the hallway of the office building. There wasn't anything special about the place, just the typical gathering of companies that didn't have anything to do with one another. Some fly by night and some more established. According to Jared's research Damian Barnes's software company was a successful one. He had twelve full-time employees and was a member of the local business association. An upstanding citizen by all accounts.

Jason found the door with the plaque next to it that read, "Barnes Financial Software, Inc." Pushing it open, he took a cursory inventory of the room behind it. On the small side, it had a few chairs for guests but most of the space was taken up by a receptionist desk that was currently empty. A glass wall behind the desk revealed even more offices and people but none of them seemed to notice his arrival.

Waiting for someone to greet him, he examined the photos on the walls. There was a large one with two men, one holding an award and the other older, maybe mid-sixties. The younger man was probably what women called handsome, but then Jason wasn't much of a judge regarding male attractiveness.

"Can I help you?"

Jason turned quickly to find a middle-aged woman standing there with a disapproving look on her face. He gave her his most charming smile, hoping to make a better impression and perhaps learn something about the elusive Damian Barnes.

"I hope you can. I'm Jason Anderson. I was hoping I could speak to Damian Barnes if he was available. I only need a few minutes of his time."

The woman sniffed, not moved at all by his debonair display. "Mr. Barnes does not see people without an appointment. Are you selling something? You can leave a business card if you like."

"No, I'm not selling anything." Jason cleared his throat, hating to reveal all the details of why he was there to someone he'd never met. He dug a business card out of his wallet and handed it to the woman. "I'm working with the Tremont Police Department to investigate a crime. We have reason to believe that Mr. Barnes might have been a witness and may have some important information."

That was kind of the truth. Damian Barnes might know much more than he realized.

The woman looked at Jason, looked at the card, and then looked back at him. "He's not here, actually. He's on vacation. He went to visit a friend in San Francisco."

Jason could believe that Barnes wasn't at home after seeing the piles of newspaper on the front porch, but he wasn't about to give in that easily.

"Does he call in? It's very important that I talk to him, ma'am. I've left messages at his home and here–"

"Yes." The receptionist nodded and placed the card on her desk. "I was the one who took those messages and I did pass them on to Mr. Barnes. He calls in every other day. I'm sure he'll contact you when he gets back into town."

Fighting his rising frustration, Jason tried one more time. "Would it be possible for me to talk to him when he calls in? Does he call at the same time of day?"

More disapproval. The dragon lady clearly didn't like being questioned.

"No, he doesn't. I'm afraid you'll just have to wait until he gets back."

Effectively cornered, Jason admitted defeat. At least for the battle but not the war.

"I'd appreciate you letting him know again that I'm anxious to speak to him. Do you know when he'll be back?"

The first crack in the woman's armor. Her smile faltered and she seemed unsure. "That I don't know. He left a few weeks ago and hasn't given a return date."

Jason whistled. "Lucky man. Thank you for your help." He turned to leave but then pointed to the framed picture on the wall. "Is that Mr. Barnes?"

The receptionist beamed with pride for her boss. "Yes, it is. He was receiving the very prestigious Alliance Award for excellence in interface design. Mr. Barnes is a brilliant man."

Barnes sure as hell didn't look much like his childhood photos. The skinny, geeky boy with thick glasses had grown into a confident man despite what he'd experienced as a youth. It was good to see he hadn't let the trauma of his past affect his future.

"I'm sure he his. Thank you and I hope to hear from him very soon. Good day."

Jason exited the office and strode down the hall, punching

the down arrow with too much force. The case was frozen in place and going nowhere fast. He'd promised Brinley he'd find this guy but things were not looking good.

Time to go back to the beginning and start again.

Chapter Twenty-Five

"I DIDN'T THINK a half wall of wallpaper would be this much work."

Brinley wiped at her damp forehead, the summer heat still blazing despite the sun beginning to set in the west. The old air conditioning unit was struggling to keep up and she'd have to look into replacing it eventually.

Right after she won the lottery or inherited a fortune from a long lost uncle.

This house was costing her every penny of her savings and she wasn't sure she even wanted it anymore since finding out her living room had hosted a dead body from an unsolved murder. She wasn't a superstitious person but it still gave her the willies. She was glad that she spent nights at Jason's house, although she'd never admit it out loud to him.

"It wasn't the wallpaper that was the pain in the ass—it was the chair rail that was the real work. Now I know what they meant when they said 'Measure twice and cut once'. They weren't kidding."

Jason took a long drink from a frosty water bottle and then lounged against a dining table leg while mopping his brow with a bandana.

"It's going to look even better when I get the floors refinished. I'm having them do all of the downstairs. I'll have to wait on the upstairs for now. Too expensive."

Jason pointed to a spot in the corner of the room near the entry to the kitchen. "You should have them look at that area over there. It makes a noise when I walk on it. Maybe they can fix it or replace those boards."

Brinley frowned and stood, walking to the corner where he'd pointed. "Here? I've never heard anything."

Jason hopped to his feet and joined her, pressing on a board with his tennis shoe. "Right here. Can you hear it?"

Brinley strained to hear what he was talking about, even kneeling down to get closer to the floor. "Jason, I can't hear anything."

"It's there. Just listen."

He walked over the boards and then back.

"Okay, I can hear a little something, but geez, you'd have to be Huck to hear it. Do you have some sort of wolf hearing?"

Jason shrugged, the muscles in his back bunching under his t-shirt and making it hard to breathe. Watching him work and sweat all day had done naughty things to her libido.

"You develop the senses you need in the dark. Listening was important."

Crap. He had that serious, intense expression back. She should have known it had to do with when he was in captivity. Wanting him happy and playful again, she changed the subject, hoping it wasn't too late.

"I'll point it out to them but the house is old. I may have to live with it." She threw her arms around his neck and smiled up at him. "I couldn't have done this without you. Dinner is on me tonight."

"I needed to take a day off from this case and decompress." Jason patted her bottom and grabbed another water bottle from the dining table. "We're spinning our wheels and it's starting to piss me off."

Brinley wiped her hands on a towel and then stepped back to survey their work from a distance. "This looks really amazing and I'm grateful that you decided to spend your day off helping me."

The dining room looked better than she had originally envisioned. The brown and gold striped wallpaper on the bottom half of the wall went perfectly with the cream color she'd painted last week. It was the perfect backdrop for the dark oak dining table and chairs that had once been her grandmother's. Add in the cafe au lait colored drapes and the room was almost perfection.

"I can be handy around the house every now and then." Jason's eyes were twinkling with mirth, his earlier mood quickly forgotten. "And as for dinner, I have that handled too. We're having a picnic under the stars."

Brinley's brows shot up. "A picnic? You had time to sneak out today and prepare food when I wasn't looking? You are talented."

"When have you ever seen me cook?" Jason snorted. "Before I met you I lived on take out, cereal, and frozen waffles—that is if I couldn't scrounge a meal at my mom and dad's. No, I ordered our dinner this morning before we got started. It should be here in about an hour which leaves us plenty of time to shower up."

Now that was a tantalizing thought. Brinley was all about being squeaky clean when Jason was the one scrubbing her back.

"Do you think there will be enough hot water for both of us?" Brinley looked up at him from beneath her lashes. For the most part she sucked at flirting but clearly Jason got the message. His lips twitched, trying to suppress what she assumed was laughter.

"Running out would be a problem. Maybe we should shower together to make sure." He actually had the nerve to waggle his eyebrows and give her a wolfish smile. "Last one in the shower has to do the dishes after dinner."

Of course she was going to lose. Jason sprinted off while she quickly locked the door and turned off the lights. Logan would be staying there again tonight but right now he was visiting a friend in Springwood and wouldn't be back until around nine.

Which meant that she and Jason would be alone for awhile.

By the time she reached the bathroom after giving Huck a cuddle, Jason was already under the steamy spray singing a Bruce Springsteen song at the top of his lungs. And doing a darn good job of it. She shed her clothes as quickly as possible and slipped into the shower behind him, wrapping her arms around his waist and pressing her face to his muscled back.

She let her hands trail down his ridged abdomen before encircling his already hard cock with her greedy fingers.

"Shit," he hissed. "That feels good. But don't think you're going to get out of doing the dishes, young lady."

Tightening her grip, she began to move her hands up and

down while nipping at the damp flesh of his back. His cock swelled even larger under her ministrations and he had to place a hand on the tiled wall to brace himself. "Are you sure?"

She heard him suck in a breath and then a groan. "Honey, I'm not even sure of my own damn name when you do that. After the other night you should remember that payback is a bitch."

Brinley remembered the evening well. Jason had kept her on the edge of orgasm with his fingers and tongue for what seemed like hours before letting her go over. What had followed had been the most intense pleasure of her life but she wasn't sure she could take that every single time they made love. She was far too needy to be able to wait that long.

"No teasing tonight." Brinley wriggled from his back to his front so they were face to face. "I can't wait that long."

Jason's rough hands massaged her bottom as the warm spray ran over their bodies, amping up her arousal. "I thought you enjoyed the other night. I know I did."

Her fingers glided up his arms to his wide shoulders. "I did. Very much. But I need you now. Any complaints about that?"

He chuckled and leaned down to kiss her neck, nuzzling at a sensitive spot behind her ear until she was sighing and grinding against his large frame. His cock was trapped between their bodies, a rod of steel pressed into the softness of her belly.

"Not a one. The truth is I don't think I can wait either. I can't keep my hands off of you."

Thank heaven for that. It felt like those magic fingers were everywhere at once. Pinching and caressing her nipples and then sliding through her already drenched slit, circling her swollen clit. Waves of heat swept over her flesh like a wildfire through the prairie.

Her hips bucked underneath his hands as she climbed ever closer to the top. In the humid confines of the shower it felt like they were the only two people in the world, insulated from all the worries and problems weighing on her shoulders. Here in this place she could forget all of that and just be a woman with her man.

Pressing her back to the cool tile, Jason lifted her effortlessly in his arms. Her feet no longer touched the ground but she trusted him implicitly to keep her from harm. His head dipped and he captured a nipple in his mouth, sucking it in deep and then scraping the sides lightly with his teeth until she was trembling in his arms.

Her nails dug into the muscles of his back, her breathing short and labored. "Now, Jason. Please now."

He didn't make her wait, lining up his cock and plunging deep with the first thrust. Brinley cried out at the beauty of being so sublimely filled as she wrapped her legs around his waist. Her forehead resting on his, the room started to spin and arrows of pleasure headed straight to her clit as he began to move. Each stroke rubbed her g-spot even as the cascade of water sluiced over her overheated flesh. The double sensations quickly sent her straight to the top and she whispered hot words of encouragement in his ear.

Feeling his fingers tighten on her hips, he thrust harder and faster, pinning her to the wall until she couldn't breathe, could barely catch her breath. She was on fire from the inside out and would happily turn to ash in his strong arms.

When her climax hit the world seemed to shatter into thousands of pieces. Light and color danced behind her lids as Jason thrust one last time before growling his own release. Her whole body tightened painfully but the pleasure washing over her was too good. Too intense.

She watched fascinated as Jason came down to earth with her, his features relaxing into a smile of satisfaction. He looked sated, his eyes heavy-lidded but still taking in every detail of her shattered appearance – her messy hair, swollen lips, and love bites on her skin that would surely turn into bruises. The damn alpha male knew what havoc he'd created and would probably strut around if she let him.

Who was she kidding? She wanted to strut too. The sex had been that brilliantly good.

She clung to him as he lowered her onto the tile, her legs still shaking from her shattering orgasm. Cuddling her close and whispering silly romantic words, he held her until her breathing returned to normal. But it was her heart that still ached painfully.

She was in love with Jason.

It wasn't simply lust or friendship but something much deeper and infinitely more wonderful if he felt the same. He clearly cared for her but was it enough? Could it grow into something that would last? She wanted a lifetime with him.

She was willing to go out on a limb and find out. She'd heard the saying that faint heart never won fair lady. Well, hell, it was probably the same in reverse. If she wanted something – someone – she had to stand up and go for it. She'd been playing it safe for too long.

He was worth it.

Chapter Twenty-Six

JASON LAID BACK on the blanket and pillowed his head on his hands, his stomach pleasantly full. After their hot sex in the shower, they'd reluctantly dressed and set up their picnic in the backyard. He'd ordered from the local diner and they'd delivered tasty fried chicken, potato salad, rolls, and two large slices of chocolate cake. Brinley had opened a bottle of wine to go along with the meal and he was feeling a little sleepy and mellow. Other than the case being stuck, today had been a good day.

Brinley rolled over and pillowed her head on his shoulder, throwing an arm over his middle. "You're quiet. Is everything okay?"

"Too much good food and wine. Not to mention the great sex before," Jason chuckled, letting his fingers play in her long, silky hair. "I think I need a nap. I'm not as young as I used to be."

Jason's fortieth birthday had come and gone a few months ago while Brinley had just passed her thirtieth. It was another obstacle, although not insurmountable. He had friends who had married women that were several years younger and so far those couples were completely happy.

Whoa.

Where had that thought come from?

He wasn't going to marry Brinley…or anyone. He had too many scars, mostly internal, to ever tie someone to him for a lifetime. He had nightmares and he couldn't even get a decent night's sleep. Hardly husband or father material.

"You're not old. Age is just a number. It's all in how you feel."

Then I feel about seventy.

"I think I'm out of shape. Working on the dining room kicked my ass today. I admire the fact that you've done so much on your own."

"I don't mind. But I'd like to have as much done as possible before school starts. I won't have any time then. I've been lucky that Logan likes home improvement. He's helped a lot."

Jason rolled onto his side so he could see her face. "That reminds me. Logan mentioned that your ex Greg has been coming by uninvited and bothering you. Do I need to have a talk with him?"

Brinley rolled her eyes. "I'd hardly call him my ex. We barely dated and we never kissed. He's more of an acquaintance that never made it to the next step. Honestly, he's kind of a jerk."

Jason had never met this Greg but he didn't like him one bit. And that didn't have anything to do with being jealous or anything. He simply sounded like a real piece of work.

"Maybe he and I should have a chat. I can let him know how things are."

Brinley ran her finger up his arm, sending tingles to parts in a southerly direction. Suddenly he wasn't all that tired anymore.

"And how are things? What would you tell him?"

She was looking up at him expectantly, and he knew what she wanted him to say. He wasn't a stupid man, although the nuances of relationships were sometimes beyond his understanding. But he'd have to be an idiot not to feel the growing bond between the two of them. She was becoming ever more important to him with each new day and it appeared she felt the same.

He had to put a stop to it now. He'd been wimping out, putting off the discussion but the time to act was here. He couldn't let her go on thinking there was a future between them. He had a shitload of work to do before he'd be ready to be someone's husband or father.

"I'd tell him to wait for an invitation, and I'd make sure he heard the words. I can be very persuasive when I want to be."

"I've already told him all that. I don't think he cares much about what's polite."

"I can make an impression that he won't forget."

Jason sat up and stretched. The very thought of this Greg guy putting his hands on Brinley made Jason want to punch the ex right in the jaw. He was possessive of her and that was a mistake. Eventually she'd date someone else and he'd have to deal with it.

And he had no clue how he was going to do that.

"If he comes by again I'll just tell him that I'm seeing someone."

The moment was here. Now.

"Look…Brinley…I think we should talk about what's going on between us and where you think this is going. I don't want there to be any misunderstandings. I want to be clear about things."

She went stiff next to him and he winced at the harshness of his words, if not the tone. A part of him wanted to backtrack and tell her he'd misspoke and that everything was okay. A bigger part of him knew that it was because he felt so much for her that he couldn't allow her to settle for less than she deserved.

"Yes, we should be clear." Her words were stilted and her expression had gone from flirtatious to icy.

Jason pressed his larger hand on her smaller one, trying to cushion the blow that he was about to inflict. This was going to hurt her but it was better to do a small hurt now than to make her a victim the rest of her life.

"I really care about you and it's because of those feelings that I say this. I've got problems, honey. We both know that. Hell, I can't even get a decent night's sleep most days. I have nightmares and there are times when I'm back in that cell. It's real to me and it may always be. I can't ask you to take all that on. Not right now. I just can't make any kind of commitment."

He expected tears and maybe some histrionics about being led on which wouldn't have been a stretch. He'd very deliberately not thought about the future when they'd started seeing each other. And sleeping together.

Instead he saw anger light up her hazel eyes. She sat up and snatched her hand back as if she'd been burnt and she held it to her chest as her lips began to tremble. The color was high in her cheeks and her spine ramrod straight.

"I don't remember asking you for a commitment, so you'll have to forgive me if I'm confused. I thought we had something special between us but I wasn't thinking that we were going to elope this weekend. I get that you're working through some things, Jason, but you don't think I understand that. I never realized your opinion of me was that low."

"It's not. I think you're terrific." Jason was astonished at her reaction. She couldn't possibly think he thought so little of her. She was amazing and wonderful.

"But not wonderful enough." Bitterness tinged her words and he knew he'd screwed this up royally. "You're a coward, Jason Anderson. I know you have feelings for me, and I darn well know I'm in love with you, but you're going to keep pushing me away. Why? Because you're scared. You're shaking in your expensive cowboy boots. Making excuses about commitments and not sleeping at night. Do you even hear yourself?"

He certainly heard her, despite the fact that she was so furious her voice had dropped to a whisper. "I'm broken inside, and you deserve better than that. You should have a man that doesn't go back to the dark place all the time."

Brinley jumped to her feet, anger in every line of her body.

"I'll take that under advisement. Just so you know, right now you're not my favorite person. You're pissing me off and I'm losing my patience. You're not putting distance between us because of your nightmares. You're doing it because you're a lily-livered chicken shit. But I get that sometimes people can be scared of their emotions so I'm going to let this pass and forget that we ever had this conversation."

Frustrated that an evening that had started so promising had turned to hell, Jason levered to his feet and tried to hold her hand but she pulled it away and shook her head.

"I feel more for you than I've ever felt for anyone but I can't guarantee that we have a future together. I can't say for sure that everything is going to be alright."

"I haven't asked for a guarantee, Jason, and do you know why? Because they don't exist. I can't give you one either but you don't hear me pussy-footing around saying things like I feel more for you than anyone else. That's a cop out. I've told you I love you and I'm not taking it back, but right now I'm deeply questioning my taste in men."

With that Brinley turned on her heel and marched into the house without a backward glance over her shoulder, leaving him standing there like a total loser.

Somewhere along the way he'd taken a wrong turn but he didn't know where. The words hadn't come out quite right and he'd first hurt her and then angered her. He'd only been trying to be honest.

And he didn't have a clue how to put things right.

Chapter Twenty-Seven

BRINLEY WAS STILL frustrated early the next morning, although the anger had faded as she readied to go out for a bicycle ride. A long one. She needed to work off the emotions that had kept her up most of the night tossing and turning in the guest room. Jason was scared of commitment and in a way she couldn't blame him. It wasn't something to take lightly, which was why she'd turned and left the conversation last night when she did. There were so many hurtful words she could have hurled at him but it wouldn't have helped him get over his fears any sooner. Only time could do that.

She scratched out a note and propped it up on the kitchen island. In getting out of the house before he was awake she hoped to avoid some of the hard feelings from last night. Once she cycled a few miles it would clear her head and she'd know what to do about the entire situation.

She grabbed a water bottle and quietly exited the house. After unlocking her bike from the front porch and pulling on her helmet, she climbed on and pedaled away, the physical exertion exactly what she needed.

The wind whipped at her long hair and instantly dried the

sweat on her skin as she built up speed, putting miles between her and her troubles. This was one of her favorite routes with all the quiet back roads and the homes few and far between. She didn't have to worry about traffic or even people. All she had to do was lose herself in the rhythm of the ride.

The cobwebs in her brain slowly lifted as her adrenaline soared. Every pump of her legs brought her closer to what she knew to be the truth.

Jason cared about her. He couldn't hide it. He probably loved her although she doubted he'd ever used that word before. The stubborn mule of a man was a confirmed bachelor and he wasn't going to fall easily. Strangely enough, he'd obviously been thinking more about the future and commitment than she had. She'd been happy to just be with him and enjoy what they had in the present. Now he was running scared.

From himself. What she really needed to do was sit back and let him deal with his internal demons. There wasn't anything she could do about them anyway except not put any more pressure on him. He'd either come to admit his love or not, and she had to be prepared either way.

But she wouldn't be passive in all this. She was done with that. She'd taken a chance and found an amazing man. She'd stick by him while he fought his battle and let him know that she was there and wasn't frightened.

The growl of an engine behind her interrupted her train of thought, and she rode even farther right to give the car as much of the full road as she could. Normally they slowed down as they went around her and waved before gunning the motor and moving on. Everyone was quite courteous to cyclists although she'd noticed that there weren't many of her kind riding around. In Chicago she'd a few accidents with some less than pleasant drivers, including one where someone had pulled in front of her and she'd gone ass over tea kettle into the dirt, breaking her wrist. That person had had the nerve to yell at Brinley for being "in the way".

She waited for the car to pass her but it didn't, perhaps waiting for a car to go by in the opposite direction. Or maybe the driver was texting. Brinley had learned to fear those people. They never seemed to pay attention to what was happening around them.

She craned her neck but couldn't see any vehicle coming toward her that would impede the car behind from going around. Pedaling even faster, she pulled as far to the right as she dared without getting into the soft shoulder that would surely toss her from the bike. Now there was no reason for the vehicle not to pass her.

Sweat trickling down her back, she heard the roar of the engine and then felt a sickening jolt that tossed her into the air like the matador at a bullfight who had connected with the horned end of the animal. Fear rippled through her as she landed like a rag doll onto the pavement with a sickening jolt that rattled her teeth and bones. The first thing she registered was the pain in her legs, arms, and torso. The second was that gravel had dug into her exposed skin and dirt and blood dripped down her knees and palms. Dazed, she reached up and felt her helmet still in place and said a small prayer of thanks that it had protected her head even as the rest of her body had borne the brunt of the collision.

Anger surged through her tangled and bruised body. She'd given the driver more than enough room to go around her. Anyone who managed to hit her under those conditions with a deserted road and clear skies was a blooming idiot who shouldn't have a license. As soon as she felt better she was going to give the driver a piece of her mind.

The car had come to a stop about ten feet ahead and was now just sitting there idling. Even in the other two accidents she'd been in the drivers had flown out of their cars to see if she was injured. The snippy one had even followed Brinley to the hospital to make sure she was okay. Now this asshole was just sitting there waiting for her to get up and climb back on her mangled bike.

What a jerk.

She waved her arm to try and get the driver's attention but she couldn't see him or her and she wasn't sure they could see her from this angle.

"Hello?" she called out, her voice weak and shaky and her breath still shallow. The excruciating pain on her right side was making it difficult to get a lungful of air. "Can you help me? I think I'm hurt."

Her bicycle lay about three feet away and the back wheel looked bent and damaged beyond repair. Even if she hadn't been hurt she wouldn't be riding it anywhere. She had her phone in the pack around her waist and she should probably just call and have someone pick her up since right now she didn't trust herself to be civil to the guy who had knocked her off her bike.

The driver still didn't answer and Brinley was losing patience. She was sprawled on the road, in pain, pissed off. This accident was their fault and by God they needed to own up to it. With her luck it was probably some teenager that was now panicking and calling mommy or daddy asking what to do. Quickly she memorized the license plate in case the car drove off without helping. It hadn't ever happened to her but hit and run wasn't unheard of.

If she could get to the driver's window she could force the person to acknowledge the incident whether they liked it or not. She tried to push herself to a sitting position but her head swam and the world tilted dangerously. She fell back onto the pavement, a pain shooting up her leg that made tears well up in her eyes.

"Hello?" she yelled again, this time as loud as she could, wincing as the sound reverberated in her skull. Her right ankle and hip was beginning to throb with pain and black dots spotted her vision. "Can you please help me?"

Still no answer and that was weird. In fact, the entire situation was strange. There should have been no reason for anyone to hit her and yet they had. Now they wouldn't get out of the car to help her which was equally bizarre.

The vehicle finally lurched as the driver put it into gear. Backup lights came to life and anger morphed into fear in that instant. The driver was going to put the car into reverse and she was lying right in the path of its bone crunching wheels. Brinley sucked air into her lungs as her heart pounded like a timpani in her ears.

The accident hadn't been one at all. He'd meant to run her down and now this lunatic was going to finish the job. How annoyed he must be that she didn't die on the first try. The whole thing with the murder and the house came down to this moment. Someone might want in the house but they wanted her dead too. They'd succeed if she didn't do something.

Move!

Her limbs shaking with terror, she used her already ripped up hands and feet to drag herself toward the side of the road where she could roll down into the ditch. A shaft of stunning pain shot up her leg that almost took her breath away but she gritted her teeth, determined to ignore anything but the voice screaming in her ear to get away.

Tears leaked down her cheeks as the car engine gunned, almost splitting her skull open with the booming sound. The last bit of strength in her battered body used up, she made it to the shoulder of the road, the soft earth a cushion on her abraded flesh and rolled as far as she could down the ditch, but not nearly far enough to protect herself. She squeezed her eyes shut, not wanting to watch her own demise, but the vehicle came to a sudden squealing stop a mere foot from where she lay. The tires spun and the car peeled away from her, spitting gravel in the air, rocks and dirt pelting her as it raced down the road.

Another car seemed to come from nowhere and she didn't even have the energy to flag the driver down. Her guardian angel must have been working overtime because the vehicle stopped and the driver frantically ran over to her, kneeling down while pulling out their phone and calling 911.

"An ambulance will be here in a minute, young lady," the elderly man said, patting her hand. "Just stay still and try not to move. What happened? Did you fall?"

Brinley shook her head and winced at the pain in her shoulders and back. She felt like she'd been beaten with a baseball bat and by someone who knew how. She'd be feeling this for days. "That car that just left hit me."

The man's bushy brows shot up. "Hit and run? I wish I'd gotten the jerk's plate number."

"I got it." She looked up into the man's kindly eyes as her vision blurred and the dark spots showed up again. "I got the number."

Brinley tried to keep her eyes open but the effort was simply too much. She let the blackness take over, shutting out the pain and fear, not wanting to even contemplate what she'd have to face when she woke up.

Things had gone from bad to really and truly awful.

✦ ✦ ✦

ADRENALINE PUMPED THROUGH Jason's veins as he launched through the emergency room entrance and straight up to the front desk. Since receiving West's phone call fifteen minutes ago, Jason had been in panic mode. Someone had tried to kill Brinley and had almost succeeded.

He hadn't been there to protect her and that was his fault. He'd heard her moving around this morning and getting ready for her ride but he'd stayed in bed like the coward he was, not wanting to deal with the issue hanging between them.

Brinley was right. He was a chicken-shit.

He'd been using his past as a shield because he was afraid of love and committing to one person. Hell, she hadn't even asked him about the future but he'd been miles ahead of her on that one, already worrying about something that might never even happen.

His gaze darted around the waiting room and landed on Logan who had been leaning against a wall, but on seeing Jason straightened and came to his side.

"Just relax. She's going to be okay. West is back with her getting a statement. I told him I'd wait for you out here."

His heart was beating so fast he thought it would jump out of his chest. He needed to see she was all right with his own two eyes. He needed to touch her and tell her he was a total asshole who didn't have a clue.

"Can I see her?"

"We can go back. The doctor is done and she's just waiting on discharge papers."

Jason followed Logan back amongst the bustling nurses and orderlies. Each patient area was curtained off and it offered a modicum of privacy, but he'd be glad to get her home and tucked up into bed where he could take care of her.

"She's in here." Logan pushed aside a curtain and gave the woman lying on the bed a big smile. "Didn't I tell you he'd break every speed law in this county to get to you? And here he is in record time."

Jason didn't expect much of a reception after what had gone down between them last night, so he was surprised when she gave him a trembling smile and held out her hand. He reached for it and then hesitated. Both of her palms were wrapped in white gauze and he didn't want to hurt her. Again.

Instead he gently reached for her arm, careful not to put any pressure on the delicate skin that was already turning purple and blue. Someone had tried to kill her and when he got his hands on that someone he was going to…

"Jason?" Brinley prompted, interrupting his thoughts that were becoming more pissed off as his gaze swept her head to toe, cataloging the injuries.

In addition to the bandaged hands, her right wrist and ankle were both wrapped in those stretchy bandages for support. Her skin looked like someone had taken a handful of rocks and rubbed them all over her body, gouges and cuts up and down her limbs and one high on her cheek. Anger churned in his gut and he vowed to make whoever had done this pay for their actions.

A hand landed on Jason's shoulder and he turned to see his brother West, a cell phone in his hand. "Your lady did good, brother. She got the license plate of the guy who did this. I've got a cruiser en route to the house the vehicle is registered to. We'll get him."

Everyone was waiting for Jason to say something but he couldn't seem to push words past the lump in his throat. Terrible images of an injured Brinley kept running through his mind, giving him a more horror-filled nightmare than being down in that cell. Losing this woman would be far worse.

"That's good." He finally managed to get his voice to work. "How did this happen? I mean, what happened? I only got a few details on the phone."

"That's because I only knew a few when I called." West shoved the phone back into his pocket. "Do you want to tell him or shall I?"

Brinley took a deep breath and patted the mattress next to her. "I'll tell him. Jason, why don't you sit down for a minute?

You don't look too good."

He didn't feel too good either, the acid in his stomach mixing with the coffee he'd been drinking when West called. He eased onto the side of the bed, trying not to jar her after everything she'd been through.

"Tell me. I want to hear every detail."

Then he wanted to find this guy and rip him limb from limb. Slowly.

Chapter Twenty-Eight

BRINLEY PRESSED THE off button on the television remote and leaned back into the soft pillows on Jason's bed, exhausted and sore. Every square inch of Brinley's body ached although her right side had taken the brunt of the fall. She'd sprained her ankle and her wrist, wrenched her hips and back, and abraded her skin until it felt like sandpaper. She'd whimpered and cried when the nurse had dug into her cuts to clean out the dirt and gravel, not just from the pain but from the overwhelming realization that the person who wanted her dead was still out there.

This whole nightmare wasn't over. As soon as they caught this crazy killer she was going to put that damn house up for sale. It was the cause of all of this heartache and it no longer felt like much of a dream home, other than it had led her to Jason. Now that was something good.

He'd carried her from the hospital to his truck and then into the house as if she was made of glass. He'd gently combed the dirt and snarls from her hair and brought her juice to wash down her pain pills. She'd napped on and off during the day, but used to being more active she'd quickly become bored.

She'd even managed to convince Logan to bring up the additional paperwork that Lita George had found of Anita's regarding the Barnes murder. There was no guarantee any of it would be helpful but it needed to be reviewed. Jason had talked about going back to the beginning and looking at the evidence again so she might as well help since she was laid up for the foreseeable future.

"You're supposed to be sleeping."

Jason stood in the doorway with a fresh glass of iced tea and a grilled cheese sandwich on a plate.

"I'm tired of sleeping. If I sleep all day I won't sleep tonight."

He strode in and set the plate and glass on the bedside table. "I bet you will. Those pills will see to it. Don't be a hero. You're in a lot of pain and the medication can help with that."

She reached for the glass with her left hand, wrapped in gauze, but he shook his head and carefully placed her hand back down on the mattress. He lifted the glass and held the straw to her lips so she could sip at the cool liquid, ambrosia to her dry throat.

"I made you some grilled cheese. West supervised so I think it's edible. You should have something in your stomach."

He wasn't going to let her lift a finger, instead hand feeding the toasted sandwich to her although she only nibbled at first. By the time she'd eaten half of it her stomach growled in hunger.

"This is good."

"You must be hungrier than I thought if you say that. I can bring you more if you want. Anything you want I'll get."

From the way he avoided her gaze she was pretty sure they needed to clear the air about last night. Near death experiences had a way of putting things into perspective. She only wished her head wasn't so fuzzy from the medication, but on the bright side it lowered her inhibitions.

"I'm not angry anymore." She swallowed the last bite and let him feed her more iced tea to wash it down. "I had time to think this morning before I was hit and I'd decided to back off and let you figure things out for yourself. But I'm not going anywhere. I'm just not going to put any pressure on you to declare feelings you're obviously not ready for."

"Jesus, I don't deserve you." Jason set the glass on the table and softly cupped her face with his large hands, setting her heart into overdrive. It was always this way with him. One touch and she was lost. "I had some time to think too. I was a gigantic asshole last night. You were right about me being scared and using what happened to me as an excuse. I do have some issues that I have to work out. The nightmares. The sleeping. But that's no reason not to beg you to love me. Because I do love you."

Awash in love and tenderness, her vision blurred with tears and her hands shook as her fingers ran down a stubbly cheek. She hadn't known him long and the words shouldn't have been that powerful, but they'd turned her world upside down. Her heart ached with emotions so strong she couldn't even begin to name them; she only knew they were good and right.

"Thank you for saying it." Her voice was choked but she managed to smile through the few tears that were falling down her cheeks. It had been too emotional a day and she was feeling the effects. "I would have waited, you know."

"I'm sorry you had to wait this long. I'm just sorry for acting stupid, saying shit to push you away. You've made the last few weeks the happiest I can remember in a long time."

"I'm not pushing here." She needed to make him understand. "Let's take this as slow as we need to. There's no hurry. We've both come with baggage and we haven't known each other long. I want you to know I have no expectations."

Jason chuckled and gave her a wide grin. "Really? Because I do. I expect that I'm going to screw up more than once and you're going to have to forgive me again."

"I think I can do that. Are you coming to bed? Where's Logan and West?"

"West went back to the office." Jason's smile fell. "The license plate you saw was on a stolen vehicle, so that was a dead end. But we're going to get this guy, honey, don't you worry. You – and your house – are going to have round the clock protection. In fact, Logan's over there now settling in for the night."

Brinley pressed her fingers to her throbbing temple, disappointment making the tears start all over again. She should have known it was too good to be true and that the killer wouldn't make such a trivial mistake.

"I feel so badly that he's been away from his wife for so long."

"She's finishing up a book, so when he's done here they're going to take the twins and head to Seattle for some fun. He'll make it up to her." He lifted her chin so she was looking into his eyes. "Are you going to be okay? I'm not talking about your cuts and bruises, honey."

"I'm fine. Really, I am."

She wasn't quite but she would be. This case wasn't going to beat her. They would find who was doing this and put them behind bars. She'd overheard Logan and Jason talking when she was supposed to be asleep and they'd said that the brazen attempt on her life meant the killer was getting desperate. Desperate men made mistakes and that was a positive development.

Jason stood and picked up the dishes. "If you're sure. I'm going downstairs for a few minutes to clean up. I'll be back with your pill and then maybe we can watch a movie or something."

He leaned down and dropped a kiss on her forehead, the only place that wasn't scratched or bruised, before bounding down the stairs. Brinley reached for the thick file folder of Anita's papers and idly paged through them. She couldn't begin to move forward with her life until this case was solved.

After all, it was her ass on the line.

✦ ✦ ✦

JASON SHIFTED THE file folder on his legs and stretched his back and shoulders, careful not to wake the sleeping woman beside him. Brinley had dozed off in the middle of the movie thanks to a couple of pain pills, but as usual he was having trouble falling asleep. To pass the time he'd started examining the file that Lita had found in her apartment. West had retrieved it but with the incident with Brinley yesterday no one had been able to give it much time.

Brinley had started to but she'd been so tired she hadn't been able to keep her eyes open long enough to make a dent in the paperwork. She'd said it was pretty much a repeat of what they'd already seen.

There were copies of the statements from the police file from all the relevant players – Wendell, Gail, and Damian. When Anita recovered, Jason would have to ask her how they got their hands on these.

There was an interesting drawing that perhaps Anita or Roger had made of the crime scene depicting where the body was located and then another of the surrounding area where Wendell was found by the police, complete with estimated driving times from the house to the lake and back.

Wendell could have easily committed the murder. He had ample opportunity and motive, plus the strange act of recreating his life with Linda – perhaps out of guilt. Love and hate were strong emotions and closely related enough for Wendell to have acted in a frenzy of passion.

That's what the case came down to. Supposition. Hunches. Theories.

None of that was going to protect Brinley's life.

He wouldn't sleep a wink tonight so he might as well go downstairs and make a pot of coffee. He'd spend the hours until morning reviewing every piece of evidence they had. Slowly he levered up from the bed, trying not to shake the mattress although Brinley was deeply asleep and probably wouldn't stir even if he made a racket. He picked up the file from the bed and tiptoed across the bedroom, cursing when a scrap of paper fell from the folder and fluttered to the floor.

Snatching it up, he made his way downstairs and into the kitchen, starting a pot of coffee and settling at the island. The small piece of paper was still in his hand and he flipped on an overhead light to examine it. The half sheet looked like it had been torn from a yellow legal pad and had a note scratched in black pen. Slipping on his glasses, he was able to make out the words more easily.

Need to talk to D. Barnes and friends.

Cop said alibi seems solid.

Jason read and re-read the note, something he couldn't put his finger on bugging him, niggling in the back of his brain, the word "seems" jumping out at him. That's how everyone's alibi started out. They all seemed plausible. It was up to the investigator to make sure it was bulletproof. Beyond question. At least until the criminal was caught. A shaky alibi didn't mean someone was guilty, but it also didn't mean they could be omitted as a suspect either.

Had the cops twenty years ago simply assumed Damian Barnes's alibi was strong? Because he was a kid? Anita and Roger couldn't have talked to the investigating officer because he had passed away five years ago, so they could only be working off of the reports.

Jason reached behind him for the police file stacked on the kitchen table and plopped it down, flipping through it looking for Damian's statement. He'd been at the movies with his friends. That seemed conclusive.

There was that word again.

The detective had a short report where he'd talked to the teenagers and they'd confirmed the four of them had all seen the seven-fifteen *Braveheart.* It was the film's opening night and they'd been talking about going for weeks. They'd even waited in line for almost two hours and the theatre had been packed.

Jason had been at college at the time but he and his friends had also gone to see *Braveheart* on opening night in their own city. He too had waited in line and the theatre had sold out. When it came time to find a place to sit, the group of ten young men had to split up because the seats left were only singles and a few doubles. After the movie, they'd regrouped in the lobby and headed out for pizza and beer.

Son of a bitch. Had anyone bothered to ask those boys if they had all sat together for the entire three hours plus previews? If Damian Barnes had sat separately he would have had plenty of time to slip out, commit the murder, then slip back in to see the end of the film and meet back up with his friends.

Jason needed to talk to those young men and a quick glance at the clock on the wall told him that it would be indecent to phone this late at night. Shit. He'd have to wait until morning. The one decent idea he'd had in days and now he had to sit on his hands for the next seven to eight hours.

Wait. Jared had sent him the current phone numbers and addresses of Damian's friends. Jason hopped off the bar stool and waded through the files on the kitchen table until he found the right one. A quick check to confirm his memory and he was grinning like an idiot. Fred March had moved out to Hawaii after graduation to manage a hotel.

Adrenaline surged through Jason's veins and that little voice was telling him this meant something. His gut agreed.

And it was only eight o'clock in the evening in Honolulu.

Chapter Twenty-Nine

"I DON'T LIKE this one bit," groused Jason as he, West, and Jared took up their designated places in Brinley's home. "She could get hurt."

"She's not going to get hurt." West settled next to Jason in the entryway closet, the door partially open so they had an unobstructed view of the living and dining room. "We walked her in the front door and then snuck her out the back under the cover of darkness and into the garage where Logan is keeping her tucked up and safe until this is all over. Hopefully we won't have to do this every night for a week."

They'd already staked out Brinley's house for the last two nights waiting for Damian Barnes – at least they assumed it was going to be Damian – to show up. After Jason had talked to Damian's friends from the movie he'd found his hunch was correct. The boys had been forced to separate and Damian had sat near the back, all alone. He'd had plenty of time to leave, shoot his stepmother, and then return to the theatre. The boys had answered the cops' questions honestly; they simply hadn't been asked the right question.

Jared had also dug up financial information that gave Damian a clear motive to getting rid of Linda Barnes. She was spending his inheritance and Wendell had changed his will so that if he died Linda would get a cut of the estate right out from under Damian.

Add in the fact that he disappeared a few weeks ago just before Roger Gaines's murder and he was looking good as a suspect. A murderer who wanted the woman Jason loved dead.

He wasn't going to allow that to happen which was why they were here hiding in a closet. Damian had been on the run, living a lie for over twenty years and no one close to him seemed to have any idea where he currently was. The best plan they could come up with was to lure him here. If he wanted in the house and he wanted Brinley dead, logic dictated he would eventually show up to take care of what he considered loose ends.

West pressed the button on his ear piece. "Report."

His brother kept his voice low although there were only the three of them in the darkened house, along with Logan and Brinley in the garage and several cops hidden in a circle around the perimeter. If Barnes showed up they'd be ready for him.

"I've got a car coming down Alder Avenue slowly."

Jason didn't know which of West's men was reporting but finally something might be happening. He hadn't realized he lived in one of the most boring neighborhoods in the entire world until he'd sat back to watch it all night.

"It's parked and a man is getting out. Wait…now he's disappeared in between the houses."

Jason's heart sped up in his chest and he had to force himself to sit, quiet and controlled. He'd been in this situation enough times to know the drill but then there had never been so much hanging in the balance.

"Okay, this is it. No talking." West nodded to Jason. "Here we go."

There was silence except for the sound of the wind chimes on Brinley's patio moving softly in the slight evening breeze. Jason waited impatiently, his fingers finding the handle of the handgun tucked into his shoulder holster. There was a good chance Barnes was armed. They already knew he was dangerous. He'd killed two people and made attempts on two more. Jason had no expectation that the man would come quietly.

They'd left the front door locked but the large windows in the living room wide open as if Brinley wanted the night air to cool the house. Jason heard a clip-clip sound – possibly Barnes snipping the screens – and then a tall man shrouded in shadow stood in the middle of the room, holding what looked like a gun in one hand and a crowbar in the other. There was just enough moonlight coming through the sheer drapes to highlight the outline but none of his features.

Every muscle in Jason's body was coiled and ready to spring, the tension in his gut churning up acid into his throat. He waited, never taking his eyes from the figure who simply stood there for the longest time. Perhaps waiting to see if he had woken the lady of the house?

Finally the figure crept up the stairs where Jared was crouched in the hall closet. Jason's phone lit up with an incoming text.

Went into bedrm.

Jason held his breath, waiting to see what the intruder would do. Once he found Brinley's bed empty would he leave or would he do what Jason was counting on?

Checkg othr bedrm.

Hopefully Barnes wouldn't find Jared, although the closet was deep and piled high with boxes. They'd made sure of that. If someone opened the door all they'd see was clutter, not a fully trained and armed ex-lawman.

Comng dwnstrs.

This was the moment he'd been waiting for. Barnes was standing at the bottom of the stairs, paused as if not sure what to do next. He'd come for Brinley but she wasn't there.

Come on. Come on. Look for it. You know it's here. This is your chance.

Jason was frozen in place but his heart was beating so loudly he was shocked that it couldn't be heard blocks away. Sweat had begun to trickle down his back, the lack of air in the small space almost stifling. The seconds stretched and time seemed to stand still as he waited. And waited.

Finally the figure slowly crept into the dining room before shining a small flashlight on the floorboards near the entrance to the kitchen. Jason slowly expelled the breath he'd been holding, relief and exultation flooding him all at the same time. Barnes was kneeling now, using the crowbar to pull up the floorboards. Jason could see him reaching down and then another long pause before the crowbar pulled up a few more boards.

It had been too long since the last time he'd caught a criminal red-handed. But he remembered the rush as if it was only yesterday. How long had it been? Months and months and all because he'd been playing it safe. He'd been doing it with Brinley too, trying to protect himself from being hurt.

He was done with that, here and now. No more tip-toeing through life, half-assing everything. As of this moment he was back and it felt more than good. It felt like the part of him that had been missing for so long. He was finally someone that not only he could respect but that he could ask Brinley to love.

Jason quietly stood and reached around the door, flipping on the overhead lights while West and Jared, who had snuck down the stairs, pointed their guns at the intruder. Bright light filled the room and Jason blinked several times as he directed the muzzle of his handgun right at the surprised man's chest.

It would soon be all over.

✦ ✦ ✦

"WAITING SUCKS."

Brinley practically yawned the whispered words as she and Logan sat in the darkened garage on a couple of chaise lawn chairs. This is where she'd spent the last two nights, unwilling to be sequestered in Jason's house with Logan as her bodyguard. She might not be useful during a stakeout but she wasn't going to be pushed aside completely. It was her life on the line and she needed to see the man that had tried to kill her face to face. She wanted to find out if evil looked the same as everyone else or if there was something different about a person who was willing to kill a fellow human being.

"It won't be long now if someone is darting in and out of the houses around here. But if you're bored I could take you back to Jason's house so you could get some sleep," Logan offered with a quiet laugh. He was lying back as if he didn't have a care in the world but she'd learned enough about him to know he was constantly at the ready. His gun was safely in his shoulder holster but the entire garage was tricked out with motion sensors. If anyone's shadow even darkened the door loud sirens were going to go off, bringing several officers with them. "I don't think this is what the doctor had in mind when he sent you home. It can't be too easy to sleep on a lawn chair, even one as nice as this."

"I dozed off and on last night. I'm too jumpy to sleep unless I take my pills. Besides, I got a good nap in this afternoon."

She could hear Logan's low chuckle in the dim light although she couldn't see him smile. "Only because Jason carried you up the stairs. You're a stubborn one, Ms. Snow."

"He is too."

"What a pair you are then." Logan sat up and in a flash was by the one side window that looked out at the house. "The lights are blazing. They must have their man."

Brinley hopped to her feet and then winced as she landed wrong on her still tender ankle. She was battered but much better than she had been a few days ago. She didn't even wear the wrap on her ankle or wrist any longer, although the bruises were turning an ugly shade of green.

Logan turned and placed a hand on her shoulder, pressing her firmly back into the chair and putting his body between her and the door. "Sit down until I hear the all clear. It's not safe yet."

She was damn tired of all of this. Being protected might

sound romantic or interesting in the movies, but mostly it was a pain in the ass. Her independent nature rebelled at the invisible chains and walls that Jason had placed around her. It was the right thing to do but it didn't mean she had to enjoy it.

A few raps at the door and a young police officer stuck his head in. "We got him. I turned off the alarm and you're free to move around."

"Is it Damian Barnes?" she asked, standing more gingerly this time.

The cop gave her an apologetic smile. "I don't know, ma'am. I haven't heard. They'll know inside."

The officer disappeared and Logan held up his hand when she would have rushed out of the garage. "You don't have to do this, you know. You'll see who it is soon enough as you'll probably have to testify if he doesn't confess or plead out."

"I can't explain it but I just need to see him." Brinley shrugged helplessly. "I know that sounds lame but this man tried to run me over with a car. I need him to not be some faceless bogeyman that haunts my nightmares. This way he's just an asshole."

"Actually that sums it up pretty well. Just remember that when we go in there you need to stay out of the way. They'll be reading him his rights and so forth."

Brinley nodded, taking a fortifying breath. "I will. Let's do this."

With Logan by her side Brinley climbed the back porch stairs and entered her kitchen. She could see Jason, West, Jared, and several police officers milling around in her dining room along with a handcuffed man with his back to her. She moved through the doorway and closer to Jason as the man turned around, giving her a full view of his face.

"Greg! What are you doing here?" Brinley grabbed Jason's arm in panic. "This isn't Damian Barnes—this is Greg Henry. That guy that cancelled dinner and who wouldn't leave me alone."

Brinley was stiff with shock at the thought that some guy she'd had coffee with had broken into her house. Greg must have lost his mind entirely to do something that stupid.

Jason's brow shot up and his head swiveled to Greg and then back to her. "This is Damian Barnes, Brinley. I saw a picture of him in his office."

Logan came to stand next to her, his arms crossed over his chest as her muddled brain tried to process Jason's statement. "And he's also Greg. I saw him the day he came visiting here, trying to get in the house. Want to tell us about that, Barnes?"

Damian Barnes or Greg or whatever the hell is name was appeared to not be a happy man. His normally handsome features were twisted into something ugly and angry, although not near as menacing as she'd imagined a killer could be.

It turned out evil looked just like everyone else.

What a frightening fact.

Damian Barnes pressed his lips together as if talking was the very last thing on his mind, but then his skin flushed a darker red and he jerked his arm away from the uniformed cop that had been standing next to him.

"I asked you out so I could get into the house. I didn't want you. I wanted to get in here to get the gun and the jewelry. That's why I brought you the coffee and the wine I'd drugged. I wanted you to fall asleep so I could retrieve my stuff. The gun and jewelry were safely tucked away under the floor until you moved here. Where are they?"

Barnes took a step toward her and she hastily retreated still stiff with shock at finding out Greg was Damian and Damian was Greg. Jason easily blocked the handcuffed man's path, his wide shoulders and back filling her view. "You mean the gun and jewels I found three days ago when I figured out it was you that killed your stepmother? They're in the crime lab and the gun is covered in fingerprints. I'm guessing they're yours."

The angry man's mouth fell open. "How–how did you find them? How did you know they were there?"

A smile played around Jason's mouth and Brinley was sure she'd never seen him look as calm and confident as he did in this moment. Solving a crime looked very good on him indeed.

"I can thank my time in captivity for that, actually. Sitting in a cell alone for weeks heightens your sense of hearing. I walked over that spot on the floor and knew something wasn't right."

West shook his head at Barnes who appeared to still be in shock. All this time the killer had been right there in front of her eyes and no one had known. She was elated that she'd never fallen for his bullshit line and charm act.

West was jotting notes in a notebook. "So you snuck out of the movie theatre and came back to the house to shoot your stepmother? How did you know your father wouldn't be home?"

"They were arguing when I left. It was pretty much their pattern that they fought and then Dad went for a long drive and was gone most of the night. I knew I'd have plenty of time."

"So you shot her and hid the gun and jewelry?" Jason asked.

"Why jewelry? Were you trying to make it look like a robbery?"

Damian's jaw jutted out and his eyes were cold. "Those belonged to my mother, not Linda. Dad would have let her keep them but that wasn't right."

"Why did you kill her?" Brinley heard herself asking before she could stop the words from tumbling out of her mouth. "And why did you kill Roger Gaines?"

"She was spending all of Dad's money. Money that was supposed to belong to me. It wasn't fair. The way she was going through it there would have been nothing left by the time my father died."

"And Roger?" West held the pencil poised on the paper. "You were the one he was meeting at the hotel, right?"

Shrugging, Damian shook his head. "He called me wanting to talk about the murder. I couldn't have him or that other girl digging up the past."

Jason's mouth was a grim line. "And Brinley? Why did you try and kill her? If you were worried about being investigated why didn't you try to kill me or West?"

"I didn't try. At first." The man moved restlessly on his feet. "I just wanted in the house. My plan wasn't to kill her but drug her so she'd be asleep while I did what I needed to do. But then I saw that flooring van and I knew I couldn't wait. I had to stop her from pulling up the floors."

"I wasn't going to do that. I was just going to refinish them." Brinley glanced at the gaping hole in her dining room floor. "Of course now I'll have to have that patched."

"The truck said they did new floors. I couldn't take any chances. If you were dead the renovations would stop."

Logan had been silent the entire time but he was shaking his head and scowling. "Why in the hell didn't you buy the house in the first place when it was for sale and save yourself all the fuss of trying to get in and worrying about the damn floors?"

"I tried," Barnes declared, a tad too loudly. "But by the time I heard Aunt Gail had put the house on the market it had been sold. She never would have sold to me anyway. Bitch."

It was all suddenly too much for Brinley. She fell into one of her dining room chairs with a soft groan of frustration. So many people dead or injured because of one man's greed.

"So you killed your stepmother for money, right? Then you killed Roger Gaines and tried to kill Anita Hazlitt because you thought they were closing in on you. And finally you tried to kill me for a gun and some jewelry and to stop any renovations on the house. Do I have all this clear?"

Damian said something she couldn't quite make out but it sounded like a few rude words. Jason had obviously had enough because he grabbed Damian's arm, and with West on the other side they escorted Barnes to a waiting squad car.

"What happens now?" Brinley slumped in the chair and watched as the police officers slowly dispersed.

Logan nodded toward the front door. "West will take Barnes to the station and book him. They'll hold him there until he can be arraigned. They'll also question him and get a full statement for the record. I doubt he'll get bail, having admitted to a double murder and two other attempted murders. In fact, if I were him I'd take a deep breath of fresh air right now because I don't think he'll be seeing freedom for a long time—if ever."

A thought wouldn't leave her alone. "Do you think his father knew?"

"Hell, that's a good question. Maybe he did and maybe he didn't. Or maybe he knew on some level but couldn't allow himself to say it out loud."

Jared stepped forward and placed his hand lightly under her elbow. She'd just met him a few days ago but already she liked him as much as Logan, although he had a very different personality. Quieter. More cerebral where Logan was loud but intense.

"Brinley? Why don't I take you back to Jason's house and we can let Logan lock up over here when the cops are done? You look like you could use a stiff shot of whiskey."

"Wrong. I need at least two. Let's go."

She let Jared escort her out of her dream home that had turned into a nightmare, through the side yard, and straight into the home of her dream man. If she had to choose between the two, she'd choose her man every single time.

Chapter Thirty

BRINLEY HAD FINISHED her first shot of whiskey when Jason joined her in his kitchen. He pulled down a highball glass and poured himself a generous dollop of the single malt scotch before knocking it back in one gulp.

"West took him to the station and they'll get his statement." Jason refilled his glass and held out the bottle to Brinley and Jared but they both shook their heads. It turned out Brinley didn't like the taste of whiskey in the least.

Jared patted her hand and then stood from the table. "Unless you need me I'm going to get on the road to the airport. I can get a flight out and be back home to Misty and Lizzie Rose mid-morning."

Jason held out his hand to Jared. "I couldn't have done this without you. I promised you no dangerous assignments when you partnered with me and I guess I lied. I pulled you away from your computer and into field work."

Jared's rich laughter filled the room as he slapped his hat on his head. "I was never in any danger. Just this young lady." He gave Brinley a smile. "And she handled it like a champ. She's a keeper, Anderson."

Brinley giggled and shook her finger at Jason. "That's right. I'm a keeper."

Jason rolled his eyes and took another drink from the glass. "I'm well aware, honey. Believe me." He turned back to Jared, who was fishing his keys out of a bowl on the kitchen counter. "What about Logan? Is he leaving with you?"

"I'm heading next door right now to help him lock up. Then he's driving me to the airport before getting on the road back home. With any luck he'll be eating pancakes with Ava and the twins in the morning. And we should all get a good night's sleep in our own homes." Jared slapped Jason on the back and grinned. "I think we've all earned it."

Jason walked his friend and partner to the car while Brinley lounged on the couch. Now that Damian – or Greg – had been captured and the mystery solved, she and Jason had a great deal to talk about. They'd never truly discussed what the future held for the two of them.

She couldn't stop her pulse from accelerating and a zing of excitement shot up her spine. The nightmare was finally over and she and Jason could just…be together.

He came back into the house and pulled his boots off, setting them by the door before coming to sit beside her. Tugging her into his arms, he ran his hand up and down her back, lying close and not saying anything for a long while. It felt amazing to simply be close to him.

"I'm real proud of you, honey. Jared's right. I don't know too many people who would have handled the pressure of all this as well as you did. You're something else."

"Don't speak too soon. I might fall apart in the morning

when I realize we don't have to question suspects or comb through police files anymore."

Brinley was pretty sure the moment when all this was going to hit her hadn't happened yet. But it would and she hoped it wouldn't be too bad. Maybe some crying or a couple of glasses of wine. Or several pairs of new shoes.

"School will start soon. You won't have much time to dwell on this."

She had to report for pre-school year activities in three weeks. It was time to move on and this was why she'd left Chicago for a fresh start.

"I still have some time off. Maybe we could go somewhere."

Brinley held her breath waiting for his answer. He'd said the day of her accident he loved her but he hadn't said it since and she didn't want to assume anything. The fear thing might have returned in full force.

"I'd like that too. Just the two of us. I think I'd like the opportunity to prove to you that I was telling you the truth."

She didn't think Jason had ever lied to her so his statement seemed strange. "Tell me the truth about what?"

His rough fingers lifted her chin so she was looking up into those sexy green eyes. He had a goofy, mushy look on his face that made her insides tumble and dance and he brushed his lips against her own once, then twice until she thought her heart might burst with love.

"About how much I love you. I'm not sure I was convincing enough. I intend to remedy that in the next week and into the future. By Christmas I hope that you'll know how I feel deep down in your bones." His palm pressed against her chest. "And in your heart. You've brought me back to life. I was half living until you came along. I was playing it safe. It took someone remarkable to shake me up and set me straight."

She wrapped her arms around his neck in delight and couldn't keep the smile from her face. They were perfect for each other. "I was doing the same thing. Afraid to take chances. I think that's why I wasn't angry with you when you pulled away. I could see myself in you. I bet you saw yourself in me too. But we both took a wild chance and look at what we've found."

"Love." Jason leaned down to capture her lips in a kiss that said so much about how he felt. More than words, his actions spoke volumes.

"Love." She could only agree. No arguments.

Brinley had found the kind of love she hadn't been sure existed. All from the boy next door.

Love thy neighbor?

Don't mind if I do.

Epilogue

JASON PATTED THE ring in his pocket for the twentieth time that day. It was another Sunday dinner with the Anderson family but today was going to be a little different. He was planning to propose to Brinley and damn if he wasn't nervous and jumpy. Brinley loved him and he loved her so he was pretty sure she was going to say yes, but he wasn't going to take it for granted.

In the past several months she'd become an integral part of the Anderson clan and his parents adored her. Brinley had helped his mother prepare Thanksgiving dinner. The two of them had baked cookies and pies for Christmas. They'd even teamed up to collect toys for some of the needy children so they would have something from Santa under the tree.

His parents hadn't said a word to Jason but he could tell that they not only wholeheartedly approved of Brinley but were wondering when he was going to ask her to marry him. On Christmas Eve West and Travis had both come right out and asked him what he was waiting for.

West strode into the living room and headed straight for the bar, barely glancing at Jason and Travis who were already sipping a fine whiskey.

"Who put the bee in your bonnet, little brother?" Travis strolled over to the bar, only limping slightly now, his hip healing more every day.

"I signed the papers this morning. I did it." West threw back the shot of whiskey and then slapped the glass down on the bar. "I can't believe it but I did it."

Jason couldn't hold back the laughter at his brother's comical expression of angst. "It's not that bad. You're now officially running for mayor. It'll be great. We'll vote for you."

West refilled his glass. "The only reason I'm doing it is that Cavendish is evil incarnate. We have to get him out of office before he ruins this town. He's only out for himself and his cronies."

"Just relax. I know the perfect person to run your campaign." Travis lifted the glass from West's hand. "Pace yourself. The day is young."

Brinley and his mother came into the living room chatting about the upcoming snow festival and he was sure Marie Anderson had roped the younger woman into volunteering. Luckily Brinley was social in nature and didn't seem to mind.

He quickly crossed to her and put his arm around her shoulders. "Mom, do you mind if I borrow Brinley for a few minutes?"

His mother laughed as she hugged West. "Have her back for dinner. Fifteen minutes tops."

Jason led Brinley through the kitchen and into the large walk in pantry. It wasn't exactly candlelight and roses but that wasn't really the type of people they were. Brinley was more about the little things than grand romantic gestures, which was a lucky thing for him. She appreciated it when he brought her coffee in bed in the mornings or when he rubbed her feet while they watched television. He was always looking for new ways to show her how much he loved her.

"Is something wrong?" Brinley was frowning at him and he reached up to smooth her forehead.

"Nothing at all. I just wanted to talk to you."

Now that the moment was here all the words he'd practiced flew right out of his head, leaving him a tongue-tied, nervous idiot. He rubbed the back of his neck with a suddenly sweaty palm. He'd rehearsed this a hundred times but maybe he should have done it a thousand.

"You wanted to talk to me," Brinley prompted, her hazel eyes wide with concern. "Go ahead. I'm listening."

"It's just…Well, I was thinking…Hell…I love you so much, honey…You have no idea how you've changed things…"

She'd made everything better. He didn't have as much trouble sleeping at night and when that nightmare showed up she held him all night long.

"I love you too," she whispered, a smile spreading across her beautiful face. "Do you want me to help you, babe?"

He didn't have a clue how but he'd take whatever he could. No one had told him that proposing was this fraught with tension. He tugged at his too tight collar and tried to speak over the lump in his throat.

"I love you, Jason Anderson." She slid her arms around his waist and pressed her curves against his more than willing body. "And yes, I want to spend my life with you. Yes, to kids and everything. Just yes. Does that help?"

A huge surge of relief made him sag against the shelves. "I feel so stupid. How did you know? Was I that obvious?"

Laughter bubbled from her full pink lips and he couldn't stop himself from kissing her a few times before she answered.

"You were not obvious at all," she finally said when he let her up for air. "In fact, I never would have guessed if it hadn't been for the time you tried to measure my finger when you thought I was asleep. That wasn't a tip off at all. Neither was the time when you asked me if I thought women looked better in white gold, yellow gold, or platinum. That was completely in character for you."

He should have known his woman was too smart to be fooled. After all, she'd helped him catch a killer.

"So you've known for weeks? Why didn't you say something?"

"And ruin your plans for a proposal?" Her hazel eyes were twinkling with love. "No way. I wanted to see how you'd do it."

He looked around the utilitarian, unromantic kitchen pantry and pulled a face. He'd never be the hearts and flowers type no matter how hard he tried. "I guess I screwed it up. This sounded like a much better idea in my head than it was in reality."

Brinley shook her head. "A house brought us together although that home is currently for sale. I think this is just fine. We can share this with your family. I think they'll be happy for us." She stood back and clasped her hands together. "Do I get my ring now?"

Chuckling, Jason drew it from his pocket and held it up for her inspection. He'd spent hours at that damn jewelry store looking for just the right ring. If she didn't like it he'd take it right back and get something else.

"It's a heart-shaped stone set in platinum with baguettes on each side." He shuffled his feet and looked down at his boots. "I picked it out because, you know, you have my heart."

When he looked up her eyes were bright with tears and he felt that lump in his throat grow to monster size while a vise squeezed his chest until he almost couldn't breathe.

"It's beautiful. Will you put it on me?" She held out her left hand. It trembled slightly, but then so did his own as he slid the ring on her dainty finger. He didn't let go, instead bending down to press a kiss in her palm.

"I'm not going to want to wait long," he warned. "I want to marry you as soon as possible."

"I think between your mother and I we can make it happen on the first day of summer vacation. How does that sound?"

Perfect. Heavenly. The snow might blanket the ground but Brinley would always be his summer girl, kissed golden by the sun.

She'd brought light to the darkest part of his soul. She'd brought love to his world.

The End

Thank you for reading Danger Incorporated – Damsel in Danger

Sign up to be notified of Olivia's new releases:

Newsletter Sign Up

http://eepurl.com/Y6aof

About the Author

Olivia Jaymes is a wife, mother, lover of sexy romance, and caffeine addict. She lives with her husband and son in central Florida and spends her days with handsome alpha males and spunky heroines.

She is currently working on a series of full-length novels called The Cowboy Justice Association. It's a contemporary romance series about lawmen in southern Montana who work to keep the peace but can't seem to find it in their own lives in addition to the erotic romance novella series – Military Moguls.

Visit Olivia Jaymes at:
www.OliviaJaymes.com

Cowboy Justice Association

Cowboy Command

Justice Healed

Cowboy Truth

Cowboy Famous

Cowboy Cool

Imperfect Justice

The Deputies

Military Moguls

Champagne and Bullets

Diamonds and Revolvers

Caviar and Covert Ops

Emeralds, Rubies, and Camouflage

Printed in Germany
by Amazon Distribution
GmbH, Leipzig